MY EMBARRASSING DAD'S GONE VIRAL!

BY THE
BRILLIANTLY FUNNY

BEN DAVIS

ILLUSTRATED BY
MIKE LOWERY

OXFORD
UNIVERSITY PRESS

REC ●

00:14:54

THE LONGEST VIDEO I'VE EVER RECORDED

Camera on?

> Yes.

Mic levels OK?

> Test. TEST.

Yep, they're fine.

Right. This is going to be the longest video I've ever recorded, so you guys better make yourselves comfortable. I'm serious. Your bums are going to be numb by the end of this.

The thing is, a lot of people have been saying stuff about my family. Some of it's true, some of it isn't. It's time to set the record straight.

The first time I realized things had gone wrong was when Mum disappeared.

No, I don't mean she was vanished into thin air by a magician, or she was kidnapped, or anything mad like that. It's just one day, I came home from school and she wasn't there. To begin with, I just thought she'd gone to a friend's house and got held up or something, but the later it got, the more worried I became.

Her mobile number was written on a pad next to the phone. I called it, but it went straight to her voicemail. Then, I called Dad at work. He was out, showing a couple around a house. That was his job, you understand, he doesn't just go around showing people houses. That would be stupid.

Anyway, he answered and was all, 'What do you mean, your mum's not there? Maybe she's gone to the shops, or something?'

When I told him that her car was still on the drive, he went quiet. See, this was back when Dad was normal. Before he became the person you all know today.

Yeah, I know it's hard to believe, but he wasn't always like that. He was clean, polite, watched TV, and shaved every single day.

Mad, isn't it?

Anyway, I heard him excuse himself from the house-hunting couple and walk away. His voice went all quiet. 'Now, Nelson,' he goes, because that's my real name. I'm named after a bloke called Nelson Mandela. My parents were mad keen on him back in the olden days. 'Nelson,' he says, 'I want you to go upstairs and check if her clothes are still in the wardrobe.'

I didn't get it, to be honest. Why would her clothes be missing? I mean she was forever moaning about how she couldn't afford nice ones any more, but that was hardly good enough reason to throw them all out, was it?

I clomped upstairs into Mum and Dad's room. The wardrobe was open. Her clothes were all gone.

When I told Dad this, he made this really sad sighing sound and said, 'I'll be home as soon as I can, son.'

After that, nothing was ever the same again.

That felt like a proper dramatic moment, so if you want to pause me and go and have a wee or something, now would be a good time.

THIS MASSIVE SHIVER

When Dad got back, he had my sister, Mary, with him. I know. It's an old people's name. I was dead against it, to be honest. I wanted her to be called Zalrog or something cool like that. I told them being called Mary was a one-way ticket to the lead role in the Nativity play. I was wrong, by the way. They didn't do a proper Nativity last year so she played a cat. I was seven when she was born. She's five now. If you can't figure out how old that makes me, you should get a better maths teacher.

Anyway, Mum always picked Mary up from school. By the time Dad got there, she was at after-school club.

I heard the front door open. I was trying to play *Legends of Titania* in my bedroom to take my mind off things, but I couldn't get into it. I went downstairs. Mary was playing with her Peter the Pirate doll without a care in the world. Dad didn't even look at me. His tie was loose around his neck and one flap of his shirt had come out of his trousers.

I asked him what was happening but he just told me to make Mary a drink and then ran up the stairs two at a time.

I was adding water to Mary's squash when I heard the yell. It wasn't one of those big screams like you guys know him for. It was muffled—kind of like he wanted to shout but was stopping himself.

Mary looked up at me. She's got these really green eyes—just like Mum. As you can see, mine are dark brown, like my dad. I took her into the lounge and switched on the TV. Luckily, *Peter the Pirate* was on. When that show is on, she wouldn't notice if a tornado full of trumpets came blasting through the room. It was just getting to the bit where Peter unleashes his parrot Gertrude to save the day. Whenever he does that, he says, 'GET 'EM, GERTRUDE', and Mary joins in super loud.

When I got upstairs, Dad was sitting on the floor. This was weird. The swivel chair in his study was the most comfortable chair in the world. Serious. If I had that chair right now, I'd be asleep before I could finish the video.

The other weird thing was this: he was crying.

I'm sure some of you guys will have seen your parents cry before. I hadn't. It was horrible. This massive shiver ran right from my scalp to the soles of my feet. No one should ever have to see their dad cry. It's just not natural.

I had no idea what to do. I mean, what would you do?

I asked him if he wanted a cup of tea.

Yeah, I know.

Needless to say, he didn't.

Then I asked him where Mum was.

He said she'd gone to live somewhere else.

I asked him why.

He passed me a piece of paper. It said:

> Nelson and Mary,
> I am so sorry that I had to leave without saying goodbye. I couldn't face it—I'm a coward I suppose. I still love you both very much. I just need some time away.
> Love,
> Mum.

I asked Dad if she was coming back.

He said no.

Then I started crying.

I HATE MONEY

Yeah, I know I'm going to get flamed for that in the comments, but I don't care. I cried. In fact, I feel like crying now just thinking about it.

This was a problem that I had no idea how to deal with. Anything else, I could relate to computer games, because that's what I know. A kid is picking on me at school? I pretend he is a Death Dragon from *Sons of Hades II* and either get out of his way, or figure out a weakness I can exploit. I'm being chased by next door's giant dog? I pretend I'm running from police canines in *Streets of Chicago* and shimmy up a tree.

That night, I lay in my bed thinking about why Mum would leave us.

I mean, yeah, she seemed sad a lot of the time.

And she was going to her yoga club nearly every night of the week.

And the two of them did argue A LOT.

But I never expected her to just disappear like that without even saying goodbye.

I mean, what good is a lousy note?

I gave up on sleep completely so I got up and switched my Xbox on. I thought I could find the answers to these questions by blasting my way through the Margarkhan Sector online. I didn't. And chunkeee3000 from Wisconsin didn't seem in the mood to help either and set me on fire with his EternaBlaze cannon.

We didn't go to school the next day. It wasn't a planned thing, it's just we didn't feel like going and Dad didn't get up until eleven to make us. While he was still in bed, I grabbed his phone from the lounge and called every friend and distant relative that Mum might have been staying with. No one had seen her.

When Dad finally got up, he just sat in front of the TV in his pyjamas. Mary perched on the arm of the chair next to him, watching for Mum coming home. I didn't get it. Why wasn't he out there, trying to get her back?

I decided that I was going to have to be the one to make a move, so I headed to Mum's work to look for her there. She worked part-time at the Curl Up and Dye salon in town. I went in and spoke to her boss, Maureen. She said Mum quit last week.

So that was a dead end. I tried every yoga studio in town, too. I felt like Bogart Dawes in *NYC Noir,* scoping the cityscape for clues. Anyway, there was no sign of her. I needed a walkthrough.

When I got home, I scoured the internet. I tried

Facebook, Twitter, every social network there was. Even this thing called Myspace. No sign of her at all. I slammed the laptop lid shut and fired the Xbox up. I went back to Margarkhan to exact my revenge on chunkeee3000. I needed to get my aggression out. Turns out he was waiting for me and blasted me to death twenty-seven times.

That made me even more annoyed, so I went to the store and looked at how much it would cost to buy my own cannon. I didn't have enough Mercenary Dollars though. That triggered something off in my brain. I replayed all Mum and Dad's rows.

'The car needs fixing, what are we going to do?'

'How are we going to pay this bill?'

'When was the last time we were able to afford anything nice?'

There was one thing that connected all the arguments.

Money.

Fighting about money all the time.

I hate money.

Wouldn't life be better if we didn't have money? Say, if I wanted a loaf of bread or whatever, I could exchange it for favours, like sweeping drives or something.

You know what, forget it. That sounds like a pain in the bum.

I figured that Mum left us because we didn't have

enough money, and if we could get more, she would come back. Dad wasn't going to tell me why she went, so that was the best I could come up with. It made sense.

Thing is, I didn't have much. Not enough to get Mum back, anyway. In my Young Savers Account, I had a grand total of twenty-nine pounds and eight pence. Not much of a saving. I would have had more, but I persuaded Mum to let me take some out so I could buy the latest *Tech Ops* just the week before.

I gave up on gaming for the night and went back to the laptop. I Googled 'how to make money fast' but it was mainly stuff about stock markets and other things I didn't understand.

I decided to try something else. I Googled 'how to make money if you're a kid.'

This time it was mainly piddly stuff—washing cars, mowing lawns, nothing big enough to get my mum back. Then I saw a blog post. It was about Walton McGere. Now, you're on YouTube, you don't need me to tell you who Walton McGere is. He is the most famous person to make videos, ever. Last time I checked his channel, he had over ten million subscribers. And he's just a normal fifteen-year-old kid who talks about computer games. TEN MILLION!

But it was a different number that caught my eye. Apparently, every time someone watches one of his videos, he gets money from advertising. The combination of that, and merchandise, books and other stuff that has come out of it, means he is now worth HALF A MILLION DOLLARS!

Now, I didn't know what that was in pounds, but I knew it must have been a lot. Not like when we went on holiday to Hungary and I found a thousand forints on the floor and thought I'd struck it rich but then Dad told me it was actually worth about two pounds fifty.

Tell you what, though, half a million dollars for sitting in front of a camera and flapping your gums about computer games. How hard could it be?

I'd have Mum back before Christmas, no bother.

DYING OF EMBARRASSMENT

When I got up the next morning, Dad was still sitting in front of the TV. I don't think he'd even gone to bed. By this time he was watching a show called *Bushcraft with Panther Blimmington-Weltby*. He had always been a fan of it, but now he was becoming kind of obsessive. It is about this bloke who lives in the middle of nowhere in the countryside, and only eats stuff he grows or kills. He makes things out of naturally occurring materials, like slingshots from tree branches and medicines from leaves. Plus, sometimes he goes around the world and learns to survive in harsh conditions. On this one, he was in the desert, drinking water from cactuses and eating camel poo. Ugh. It put me right off my Coco Pops.

Anyway, when I realized Dad wasn't going to move, I said I'd walk Mary to school. The way I looked at it, I was just stepping up while my parents were having a bit of time off.

When we left, Dad said goodbye without taking his eyes off the screen. I noticed his face getting a little fuzzier, and he had been writing notes about Panther on a pad. I know—I should have seen the signs.

When I was at school, I didn't say anything about what was happening. I just wanted everyone to think that everything was normal. Not that my best mate Francis would have been much help, anyway. Looking back, I have no idea why we were such good friends. I mean, we had nothing in common.

I liked computer games.

He liked stamp collecting.

I liked rock music.

He liked stamp collecting.

I didn't like stamp collecting.

He really liked stamp collecting.

At break time I asked him what he knew about vlogging. He scrunched his nose up to keep his glasses on and said, 'A negligible amount.' He was always talking like that. It was kind of weird. 'But I am a fan of Humphrey Flipperton—Master Philatelist. His missives on the Purple Marshal Petain Series he picked up in Paris were extraordinary.'

Anyway, I went down to the library at lunchtime and watched some of these videos, and Humphrey, no offence, mate, but they were the most boring things I have ever seen in my life. I mean, stamps? WHO CARES? Why not collect envelopes? At least you can put stuff in them. Plus, he talks IN. THE. SAME. TONE. ALL. THE. TIME. Like some kind of dorky robot in a rubbish cardigan.

Like I said, no offence.

It made me realize that my videos needed to be really fun and lively if they were going to reach an audience beyond Francis.

I fetched Mary from school and plonked her in the lounge, where Dad was STILL watching Panther Blimmington-Weltby. By this time, he was suckling at a zebra's teat for milk. Panther I mean, not Dad.

Mary was NOT happy. Mum being gone was bad enough, but her favourite TV show being replaced by a posh weirdo wearing pants made of leaves was a step too far.

When Dad wouldn't tell her where Mum was, she came to me, demanding answers. I didn't know what to say, so I told her she had gone on holiday for a while. I figured that if I could make enough money to get her back within a couple of weeks, Mary would never have to know the truth.

Before I could start making videos, I had to pick a name for my channel. I went through obvious stuff like TechOpsDude and GamerGuy but they were taken. Then I thought I should go for something personal, which is why I ended up as Lugs.

As you can probably see, my ears kind of stick out a little more than most people. I used to get teased about it at school. Still do. So this was me taking ownership of an insult. Plus, the name was free.

Anyway, here is my first video. If you need me, I'll be dying of embarrassment.

ME: Hey, hey, peeps, Lugs here giving you the lowdown on the latest TechOps title—*ExoWar*. Let me tell you—it is AH. MAZE. ZING.

MARY: Who are you talking to?

ME: Nobody, Mary, just go back downstairs. The

graphics on this are incredible. There were times when I felt like the cyborg army was coming right at me.

MARY: Nelson, I want to watch *Peter the Pirate* but Daddy is watching a mad man doing strange things to a stripy horsey.

ME: Please, give me one minute and I'll put *Peter the Pirate* on the computer. As I was saying, there is literally nothing wrong with this title. It's even better if you can take advantage of the DLC and get the modified Thermoblaster.

MARY: Nelson?

ME: JUST SHUT UP, MARY, I'M BUSY!

Ah, come on, don't cry.

Looking back, I don't know why I uploaded it.

GOING BACK TO BASICS

I thought my super-lively approach would have pulled in the views. I woke up early the next morning and logged on—my hands were shaking.

Eight views.

I couldn't believe it. Maybe this making money out of YouTube thing wasn't going to be as easy as I thought.

Just as I was checking that there wasn't some kind of mistake, Dad came in without knocking. That was weird, he always knocked.

He nodded at my laptop and asked me what I was doing. I control-escaped the screen and said, 'Homework.'

His face went all weird and he said, 'I'm going to start restricting your use on that thing. It's not healthy. In fact, I'm not sure I like you using that internet at all. You never know what kind of predators might be lurking.'

And he just kept going on and on.

Anyway, I didn't think anything of it, guys. I just guessed he was getting a bit stressed about Mum leaving. I tried telling him about my plans to get her back, but he didn't want to hear it. If it wasn't Panther Blimmington-

Weltby, he wasn't interested. I noticed a big stack of his books sitting on the dining room table: *Introduction to Bushcraft, Embracing Your Inner Hunter, Going Back to Basics: How to Live Authentically*. I picked the last one up and flipped through it. I yawned so hard, my jaw nearly fell off.

I spent all day at school thinking about how to promote my videos but couldn't come up with anything. All my lunchtime Google research uncovered was that offensive stuff got publicity. I'm not sure I really liked that idea, but if it worked, it might have been worth a go. I started making a list of all the offensive stuff I could think of but the best I could come up with was 'Mr Bunsworthy smells like coffee and old socks' which was true, but wouldn't really reel in the views.

It was Friday so I had the weekend to think of something. By midday Saturday, I wished I was still at school.

I was just reaching a real good bit on *DungeonMaster VII* online. I had been working on video ideas all morning and decided to reward myself with a quick gaming break. I was taking on Facepunch85—

number one on the leaderboard for a whole year. He was down to his last life, and I had him cornered. One more spell, and he would be defeated and I would be number one in the country. Can you imagine how good that would be? Number one *DungeonMaster VII* player. Think of the kudos I would get from the gaming community. Kudos that I could have turned into views on my YouTube channel, and views that I could have turned into money to get my mum back. That was probably why I was playing so well, I wanted it more.

My character Marrkkron stomped over to Facepunch85. I took a deep breath and put on the scariest voice I could. I growled, 'Time to end this. Time for Marrkkron to become number—'

The screen went blank.

I screamed. Actually screamed.

I looked up and saw Dad standing next to my window holding the Xbox plug in his hand.

I had never been more furious in my life. I yelled at him, 'WHAT DID YOU DO

THAT FOR?' And he was all, 'It is a beautiful afternoon and you are stuck inside playing games. You need to get outside for some fresh air. When I was your age, I was always out playing, exploring, having adventures, not sitting inside with the curtains drawn, talking to losers on the internet.'

I was like, 'Well first of all, in your day the internet hadn't been invented. Neither had electricity probably. And second, how can Facepunch85 be a loser? He is the number one *DungeonMaster VII* player in the whole country!'

Dad just shook his head and walked out. Within seconds, I could hear the *Bushcraft with Panther Blimmington-Weltby* music. I was so angry, I actually beat my pillow, imagining it was Panther's smug face. Survive that, you poo-eating weirdo.

The next morning, I went to try and find Facepunch85 for a rematch, but I couldn't get online. I ran downstairs to find the router unplugged.

'There is a reason for that,' said Dad, never looking up from his whittling. Yeah, this was when he started with that. Apparently, he learned to do it when he was younger, but stopped when he met Mum. Now, he was picking it up again, carving ornaments out of blocks of wood. By this point he had already made a bear, two dogs, and a chicken. He said, 'Today you must go out and play. Take your sister to the park for an hour or two.'

'But Dad—'

He held up a hand to silence me and said, 'This is not up for discussion.'

So me and Mary went to the park. It was pretty boring. Mainly me pushing Mary on the swing while she yelled 'wheeeeee', and pretending to be Peter the Pirate's arch-enemy, Captain Crayfish. Doing that voice for so long really hurt my throat.

When I got back inside, I couldn't believe what I was seeing—the lounge was empty. Dad came bursting in from the kitchen, holding a box full of plates and bowls. I tried to get him to stop and explain, but he just said, 'We're changing our way of life, my dear children.'

I followed him around the house, watching him stack stuff into boxes, and demanded to know what he was going on about.

He said, 'Never mind. Just get up to your room and pack only essential items.'

I was like, 'UGH?'

He pointed at me with a wooden giraffe ornament. 'JUST DO IT! You too, Mary.'

When I saw my room I thought I was going to pass out. It looked like I'd been burgled. My Xbox, my TV, my laptop—all gone. How was I supposed to make videos to get Mum back without my computer?

When I screamed noises that were supposed to be words at Dad, he said, 'We're downsizing. Simplifying. Going back to basics.'

I literally didn't understand anything he was saying.

I was like, 'WHERE IS MY STUFF?'

He said, 'I sold it.'

Remember me saying earlier how I'd never been so angry in my entire life? Well, this just set a new record. And anyway, if he was going to flog anything, why wasn't it those Panther Blimmington-Weltby books?

Dad never stopped moving the whole time. He was like a whirlwind. The corner of the room seemed massive without the TV in it.

I said, 'Please just tell me what's happening.'

He put a potpourri bowl down and looked at me for the first time. He said, 'I'm selling the house. It holds too many bad memories and is bad for us as a family. I have secured a small property in the countryside where we will make our home from now on. I have sold all of our electrical equipment because it is toxic and harmful. We will live by the Blimmington-Weltby philosophy.'

I couldn't speak. I didn't know whether to cry or scream or what. My Mum, my stuff, and now my house were being taken away from me. It was the only place I'd ever lived. I remembered all the things that happened there. Birthdays, Christmases, the first time Mum and Dad brought Mary home. Plus, what about school? And my friends? What would Francis do? I was pretty much his only friend. Without me, he'd probably end up talking to the Queen's heads on his stamps.

I was like, 'But you can't do this.'

Dad said, 'I already have. We leave first thing tomorrow.'

'WHAT?'

Mary came running down the stairs, wanting to know what was happening.

When Dad told her, she screamed for three hours.

I AM A FREE SPIRIT

When we pulled up outside the house, Dad turned around to us and said, 'What do you think, kids? Magnificent, isn't she?'

Tell you what, guys, if you stopped me there and asked me to come up with a list of words to describe that house, magnificent would be about twelve-thousandth. Number one would probably be 'dump'.

I mean I know you've seen it already, but it was just horrible. Way worse than that stupid Panther's house. It reminded me of something off an old horror film—this run-down farmhouse in the middle of nowhere. It was dark by the time we got there because we had to keep stopping for Mary to puke or have a wee, which made it look even worse. The garden, if you could call it that, was overgrown and choked with weeds. There were these two worn-out looking little buildings around the side, too.

The whole house was covered in vines that started off green before turning brown and dying off. It was as if Mother Nature was trying to reclaim it and then saying, 'Actually, I don't want it.'

When I used to moan about kids calling me Lugs, my mum would say, 'You're beautiful on the inside and that's what counts.' Well, this house was ugly outside and in. Imagine your granny's house but a billion times older. The curtains were so tatty that I bet there were previously undiscovered species of insect living in them. I mean, I went into the kitchen and there was a spider in there the size of my head. I ran out screaming. Mary walked in, picked it up, let it crawl all over her, and named it Stanley. She's weird.

I wanted to cry and I'm not ashamed to admit it. We didn't even have beds, so we had to get in sleeping bags in front of the fire. It was a proper open fireplace, like you see in Downton Abbey and that, but you know, way crummier. It was freezing in there too, but Dad couldn't light it because there was no firewood and it was raining outside. In the end, he burned his suits. He said, 'My new job requires no uniform. From now on I work for the land.'

I wanted to reach up and rip the Dad mask off Panther Blimmington-Weltby's face. I mean, what was happening to my parents? Had they been driven mad by some kind of toxin like in *BioDisaster III*? A game I will NEVER get to complete.

I hardly slept that night, I was too worried about what kind of horrific beast could be waiting to crawl across my face and into my mouth. Stanley could have been the baby of the family for all I knew.

I must have drifted off eventually because the next thing I know, it's light and I'm being woken up by this weird scratching noise.

I sat up. I felt like I'd been punched in the spine by the Robopuncher from the Xbox game of the same name. Dad sat on a box in front of the window, whittling a sheep out of wood. By his side was a pig, a cow, and a horse.

I was like, 'Oh my God, how long have you been up?'

He said, 'I have been whittling by candlelight for some hours. This is what I do now. I whittle.'

I wondered if I had gone mad, and I was actually strapped to a bed in a looney bin somewhere, spitting at the nurses. I asked him to go into a bit more detail.

He put his work down and clasped his hands together. He said, 'As of now, I am no longer an estate agent. My soul is no longer shackled to the nine-to-five. I am a free spirit. I am a whittler.'

There was a silence that was only broken when a shelf fell off the wall.

'But what will we do for money?' I asked him. I thought there was no way Mum would come back if Dad had quit his job. We needed more money, not less.

He said, 'Once the house sale goes through, we will have enough funds to last us many years. In the meantime, we have some spare cash from the electrical goods we sold. But that doesn't matter. The reason I moved us out here is so we would be less reliant on money, and on the so-called comforts of the modern world. I know it is going to be a shock to the system, but in time, we will all be happier. I promise.'

I think he could tell we weren't convinced, but he carried on anyway.

'When your mother and I first married, I wanted to buy a place like this, but she wasn't interested. She wanted a new build. Something easy. Now, I will live my dream, and you, my children, are going to live it with me.'

I scrunched my eyes shut and imagined myself finding Panther Blimmington-Weltby out in the wilderness and feeding him to a pack of hungry lions.

Luckily, breakfast wasn't wild animal poo, but a mixture of different types of fruit. Mary started whinging because she wanted Suga Zingas. Dad saying that Suga Zingas are poison and that we would never buy them again only made her worse.

After breakfast, I explored our new house properly. It looked even crummier in the daylight. I must have searched the house from top to bottom about three hundred times before I had to ask Dad where the toilet was. The night before, I had to go number one in a bucket because I couldn't find it.

'Outside,' he said.

I couldn't have been more freaked out if he'd said, 'on the ceiling'.

I was like, 'But that's . . . outside.'

Dad shook his head and launched into this massive speech about how the children of today take for granted modern conveniences like indoor plumbing and that walking outside to use the toilet would help us to appreciate nature. You know what I would appreciate more? Not having my bum cheeks frozen to toilet seats.

And get this—there was no shower. All we had was an old rusty bath with loads of holes in it. When I asked Dad how we were supposed to get clean, he said we should have a 'personal wash' in the sink.

A personal wash.

Before I could ask what the hell a personal wash was, Dad shoved me and Mary outside. He said, 'I have many things to be getting on with in here, so you two make yourselves scarce.'

I looked around. All I could see were trees.

'And do what?'

He swept his hand around like he was pretending to clean a giant window. 'Go forth and enjoy the bounty of nature.' Then he slammed the door.

I was freaking out. I mean, WHAT THE HELL WAS HE TALKING ABOUT?

Mary tugged on my trouser leg and asked me if the bounty of nature was some kind of chocolate bar. I didn't have the heart to tell her it wasn't.

THE BOUNTY OF NATURE

We walked up the long dirt track, desperate to find something to do. There was another house further up, but that was all. It looked to be in slightly better nick than ours. Then again, a cardboard box full of old nappies would be an improvement on our house.

The dirt track led to a main road with no path. A mildew-infested sign at the side of the road said

WELCOME TO
SHEEPY MURVA
TWINNED WITH *BEIRUT*

I grabbed Mary's hand and led her down the road. The sea became visible in the distance, all grey and choppy. Mary started to get excited. She thought it was going to be like Blackpool.

'Will there be a tower? Will there be an arcade? Will there be donkeys?'

There was no tower. Unless you count an electricity pylon.

There was no arcade. Unless you count this old box where you put a pound in and it gave you a rude magazine.

There was a donkey. Sadly not for pleasure rides. There was a crazy man on the back of it, swaying and singing. Mary wanted to go over and pet it but I said maybe another time.

She wanted to pet the donkey, by the way. Not the mad bloke.

There was nothing on the seafront. No shops. No beach. No buckets and spades. Nothing. Just an old wooden shack and a few pathetic looking boats bobbing around in the filthy water.

Mary was all, 'Where is the fair? I want CANDY FLOSS!'

Her shouting alerted the attention of this old bloke in the shack. He poked his head out and yelled, 'AHOY THERE!'

Oh great, I thought, we've attracted a local weirdo. I mentally prepared myself to face him in combat like you do with the villagers from *Sleepy Hill: Bloodlust of the Mountain People*.

The old man shuffled over to us. He had a long white beard and was wearing a stained T-shirt that said **'HARBOURMASTERS: DO IT IN THE SEA.'**

He said, 'You must be the new residents of the farmhouse. Pleased to meet ya. I'm Scarfwick, the harbourmaster.'

I was about to introduce us when Scarfwick suddenly

twitched and swore. Now, I'm a family friendly vlogger, so I don't want to repeat what he actually said, so I'll just say this: imagine the worst swear word you can think of. Well, it's not that one, it's the second worst. You know the one I mean.

I clamped my hands over Mary's ears but it was too late. She'd heard it.

Scarfwick apologized and said he had a condition that made him do it. Then he said another swear word. This time it was the worst one. Yep, I was shocked, too.

I tried to change the subject by asking him if he was in charge of the boats.

He started grinning and was like, 'Oh yes, I contact every vessel that passes by these shores through me radio. Although I must admit, we don't get too many ships in the harbour these days.'

I wanted to say, 'It's probably because they think you're telling them to BLEEP off,' but I didn't. I felt kind of bad for him.

'Anyway, lad, if you ever fancy a day's work, you can get on a vessel with me and come fishing. There's good money to be made from it.'

Money. I needed money to get Mum back. And now the YouTube video idea was out of the window, maybe I could get a job. I could earn enough cash to make up for Dad losing his. I just really needed her back to save us from this horrible place.

I said OK and asked when he was next going out.

He said, 'Tomorrow. We sail at dawn.'

I agreed to do it. A few shifts on the boat, and I would be filthy rich.

When we got back home, Dad let us in with a big smile on his face. He said, 'So, my children. How was the bounty of nature?'

'BLEEP off,' said Mary.

A FINE MORNIN' FOR FISHIN'

To begin with, Dad wasn't keen on the idea of me getting on a boat with a creepy old man who'd taught his five-year-old daughter the second worst swear word in the world, but after I spun him a line about appreciating the bounty of nature and being self-sufficient like Panther Blimmington-Weltby, he let me go.

While we were out, he had got us all some mattresses. We had a bedroom each. Mine was the second biggest and looked out over the back garden. Actually, 'garden' wasn't really the right word for it. It was more like the Amazon rainforest. I didn't want to go out there in case I got eaten by a tribe of cannibals.

Dad had made some improvements around the house, too. He had built some chairs, a table, and a bookcase and had cleaned the kitchen so you were at least able to eat something in there without worrying you'd get some kind of disease.

I guessed it was all a distraction from us constantly asking him if he knew where Mum was. I even tried searching through letters and papers for clues but there was nothing.

We were struggling with the lack of technology, too. To Mary, TV was a basic essential and we might as well have been without running water. Being without games was driving me crazy, too. My thumbs twitched involuntarily and I found myself wondering if BeefBoy27 was still top of the BobSquad leaderboards.

I got up at four the next morning. Dad was already awake. I guessed he had completely given up on sleep by this point.

I asked him where he got our mattresses from, because mine was a bit lumpy. He said he found them in a skip.

After I had had a thorough 'personal wash' in the sink, I left the house and headed for the harbour. The wind was so cold, it went through my coat, jumper, T-shirt, and woolly hat.

I wrapped my arms around myself and thought about Mum coming back. As soon as our money troubles were over, we could return to our old house and go back to old times, when we were all happy. God, I missed her so much, it actually hurt.

When I got to the harbour, I couldn't believe my eyes. Back when we had a TV, Dad used to watch this show called *Trawler Kings*. It was about these tough American fishermen with names like 'Scruffy' and 'Big Pete' who would go out to sea in stormy conditions and swear and have quality banter. I was expecting Scarfwick's ship to be like the one on that—a mahoosive aircraft carrier type thing, with gigantic nets and a room with radios and computers in.

Scarfwick's boat was not like that. It was this little wooden thing. I remember years ago, I sneaked downstairs and watched this old, scary film called *Jaws*. It was about this evil, giant shark who ate loads of people. If there was a Jaws anywhere in Sheepy Murva bay, it would bite that little thing in half. The two of us would be shark poop bobbing on the waves in no time.

The thing is, you'd think Scarfwick being an old seadog would reassure me, but the old seadog was one of the first to get chewed up in that film.

Anyway, as soon as I stepped on the boat, I felt peaky. And we hadn't even moved. The only time I'd been on a boat before was when we got a ferry to Ireland this once, and I spent the whole time with my head in a bag. I just assumed that because I had completed *Buccaneers IV*, I had grown out of seasickness.

I really hadn't.

Scarfwick slapped me on the back and took a big drag of air. ''Tis a fine mornin' for fishin', young Nelson. We're going to reap a big haul, I can feel it in me bones.'

I didn't reply because I thought if I opened my mouth,

I would spew everywhere. We sailed until the shore was nothing but a faint line on the horizon. The water was brown and churning. I held onto my life jacket and shook. The boat stopping didn't make me feel better. We just kept bobbing and bobbing. Why couldn't the sea just keep still for a bit?

Scarfwick gave me a rod and told me to cast it out. It was only then I realized the problem. I had no idea how to do it. I had never been fishing in my life. Never even played a fishing game, because, come on, who would ever play such a boring thing?

Scarfwick growled. 'What do ya mean, you don't know what to do?' Then he swore. I didn't know whether that was his condition or whether he was just really angry with me.

Anyway, he showed me how to do it, then dropped a large net over the side.

I sat down and screwed my eyes shut. I thought that would stop the sicky feeling. It didn't.

'Looks like we got something in the net,' Scarfwick barked after about an hour. 'Let's reel it in.'

I stood up and tried to help, saying to myself, 'I'm not going to puke, I'm not going to puke, I'm not going to puke.'

The pulley struggled to drag the net from the horrible dirty water. Scarfwick ran to the lever and pumped it, trying to yank it out.

'Looks like we've got something big, my lad, I told you

it would be a grand harvest!'

The rope got tighter and tighter until the net finally dragged up the massive weight.

A shopping trolley.

Scarfwick's face fell. Then I puked over the side.

* * *

The rest of the day seemed to take a year to pass. We didn't speak. The only sounds were rushing waves, cawing seagulls, me puking, and Scarfwick swearing.

I didn't learn anything about fishing, but I did learn more about cursing than I had from looking at a million YouTube comments.

When we pulled back into the harbour, my skin was bright pink. I felt like my fingers were going to drop off. Plus, my stomach was burning. It was as if I had puked up every meal I had ever eaten. Still, the money was going to make it worth it and it would be a great story to tell Mum. Once she heard what I had been through for her, she would let me get away with anything.

I could almost feel the weight of the money in my hand. Sweet profit. Sweet dough. Sweet . . .

'THREE QUID?'

'Don't spend it all at once, lad,' Scarfwick said, with a wink.

'I did all that for three quid?'

He said, 'Well, we didn't catch anything. Your bellyaching must have scared them away.'

I buried my face in my hands. To save enough money to get Mum back, I would need to work on that boat for about four thousand years. I was beginning to give up hope of ever getting her back.

Later that night, I went home and wrote a note for her.
It said:

Mum (Jenny Lambsley, Atherworth, Staffordshire),

I know this is a squillion-to-one shot but it is the only thing I could think of doing.

I want you to come home to us. We all love you and miss you so much.

Mary needs you. I need you. Dad definitely needs you.

We now live at: 2 Pig Drive, Sheepy Murva, Norfolk, NR56 TRF

Love,
Nelson

YOU MEAN LIKE INTERNET?

The next morning, there was a knock at the door. I shot up and ran to it. I thought the message in the bottle had worked its magic in record time.

When I opened the door, my heart dropped. It wasn't Mum. It was a woman about her age. She had this cool big afro style hair, and had loads of different coloured bangles on her arm.

She smiled at me and said, 'Hi there, I'm Primrose, I live at the house down the lane. Are your parents home?'

I scratched the back of my head. 'Well, my dad is.'

Dad and Mary appeared either side of me. Dad said 'hello', all suspicious-like.

Primrose repeated her introduction and held her hand out for a shake. Dad took it. Eventually.

She said, 'Are you settling in OK? I know some of the locals can be a little . . .'

'Sweary?' I said.

She laughed. 'Yes, something like that. I've been here six months so have only just got used to them myself.'

Dad was like, 'We are settling in very well, thank you.'

Nobody said anything. It was proper awkward. My mind buzzed. Is Dad supposed to be inviting her in? Should I invite her in? Do I really want someone else to see what a dump our house is?

Thankfully, Primrose spoke. 'Anyway, if there's ever anything I can help you with, just let me know.'

'Thank you,' said Dad.

Primrose was like, 'Sorry, you didn't tell me your name.'

'Tim Lambsley,' said Dad, staring at the floor.

I didn't get why he was being so off with Primrose. She was trying really hard to be nice, too. He perked up when she complimented the ornaments in the window, though.

'Yes, I made them myself. It is my trade.'

Primrose was all, 'Oh how wonderful. I wish I could do something like that. You know, make something you can actually hold in your hands? It's not really my speciality though, being a web designer.'

Dad's half smile shrivelled into nothing. 'Web designer? You mean like, internet?'

Primrose smiled and frowned at the same time and said yes.

Dad went, 'Well, it was nice meeting you, Primrose but I don't think we'll be needing anything, thanks.'

Then he closed the door in her face and walked back to the kitchen.

I asked him why he was so mean to Primrose. She seemed really nice.

Dad spun around and said, 'You are to have no contact with that woman, do you understand me?'

I was shocked. I mean, what was wrong with her?

He said, 'I brought you out here to get away from that wretched internet, but it seems there is no escape. Promise me you will never go near her.' He had this really intense look on his face.

I wasn't happy about it but I promised. I had no choice.

'You promise, too,' he said to Mary.

Mary burst into tears. Dad sighed and carried her into the kitchen and offered her an apple he picked off a tree on the main road. This did not stop the tears.

CAN I GET AN UH HUH?

Dad woke us up the next morning at six thirty. He said we had to be ready to resume our education. Yep, he had apparently already enrolled us at local schools. Well, I say local, the nearest school was actually a forty-five-minute bus journey away in a town called Snessport. What a pain. Back when I was at Lowes Park, I could roll out of bed and be in class within twenty minutes.

While Mary and I ate breakfast (we had been upgraded to toast made from home-made bread) Dad was hunched over the table, writing adverts for his whittling business. He was going to put them in magazines and take orders by mail. Yes, mail. As if it's 1586 or something. Of course, any normal person would set up a website, but, as we know, my dad was becoming anything but normal. I mean, he hadn't shaved since Mum left and his beard was growing bushier by the day. Nothing like the one you guys know him for, but it was getting there.

Anyway, the bus journey was horrible. It was all twisting lanes and we kept getting stuck behind tractors. It's as if motorways haven't been invented in Norfolk yet.

We were wearing our old school uniforms, and we would pick up our new blazers and jumpers when we got there.

Dad came with us because he had to meet Mary's teacher. I wished he hadn't brought his whittling with him. His seat was covered with wood shavings.

I don't really know what I was expecting from this new place. It was called the Arthur Milichip School, which was a bit weird, but other than that, it was pretty much the same as Lowes Park. The building is this big, grey thing and there's a field. What else is there to say?

I went to reception and was given a timetable and a blazer that was miles too big. The receptionist was all, 'You'll grow into it, sweetheart.' Then, she told me my welcoming party would be coming down to receive me.

Thing is, guys, 'welcoming party' made it sound like there was going to be a big conga line with jelly and ice cream and stuff. It was kind of misleading. It was actually just two kids from my form called Ash and Kirsty.

The main thing I remember on first meeting them was how much taller Kirsty was than either of us. It was quite embarrassing, really. She had long, ginger hair and these really thick glasses, too. Ash seemed kind of awkward and would never look me in the eye. Neither of them seemed like they could be bothered to be my welcoming party. It was all, 'Yeah, this is the canteen, these are the toilets, this is the sports hall.'

It turns out they'd been made to hang around with me for the first week or so, so I would know where I was going. It was proper three's a crowd.

When we got to our form room, I sat with them at the back. Other kids were staring at me. I felt bad but then I remembered that whenever a new kid started at my old school, I'd probably stared just as much.

Our form teacher, Mr Tronk, walked in and I nearly started laughing. He had this massive greasy quiff and loads of rings on his fingers. He even wore a leather jacket. He was clearly trying to look like that old, dead singer Elvis Presley.

When he saw me he clicked his fingers and pointed at me with a pistol-shaped hand. 'Nice to meet ya, new kid.' That is really how he talked. In that strange kind of American accent. I was surprised because I thought it was against the law for mentalists to be teachers.

Again, sorry if you're watching this, Mr Tronk, but I have to keep it real at all times. I owe it to my subscribers.

Anyway, he beckoned me to the front of the class and draped his ruby-ringed hand over my shoulder. He said, 'Now then, boys and girls, this here's Nelson Lambsley. He's come to us from them Middle lands. Now, I want you to make young Nelson here as welcome as possible. Can I get an uh huh?'

The class did the most half-hearted 'uh huh' I'd ever heard in my life. Thinking about it, I'm pretty sure it was the only 'uh huh' I'd heard in my life.

'I SAID, CAN I GET AN UH HUH?' he yelled.

The class managed a slightly better one that time.

He said, 'Thankyouverymuch.'

It turned out that not only was Tronk our form tutor, but he was also our English teacher. And he gave us homework straight away—we had to do a report about the period when Shakespeare was writing. It wasn't until I left the class that I realized I had no way of actually doing any research at home.

I hung around with Ash and Kirsty at lunch. They were kind of just talking to each other and not me. It was a bit weird. I wanted to start up a conversation, but I couldn't think of anything to say. Once you've commented on the quality of the chips, you kind of run out of steam.

I realized I had a little bit of change left over from dinner, enough to buy a couple of chocolate bars. Ohhhh. Chocolate. I know I'd only been without it for a few days, but it felt like years. I remembered there was a little shop up the road by the bus stop. I decided to go up there before the end of lunch. I know I could have waited until the end of the day, but it was a nice break in the awkwardness. Plus, I really needed that chocolate.

I was about to step into the shop when someone coming the other way blocked my path. I looked up and gulped. He was wearing an Arthur Milichip uniform, but was way bigger than me. He held a bunch of flowers in his enormous gorilla hands. I panicked and said, 'Oh I know it's my first day, but you shouldn't have.'

He did NOT laugh.

I tried to step around him, but he was still somehow in my way. He was literally like a wall. He grunted 'new kid' at me. I said, 'Yep, certainly am,' and tried again to enter the shop. This time, he grabbed me by the collar and dragged me into the bus shelter.

He got right in my face and said, 'Do you know who I am?'

I shook my head.

He said, 'The name's Marshall Cremaine. Everyone knows who I am.'

It was as if he was some kind of really huge, scary celebrity. He said to me, 'You're going to do me a favour, new kid.'

My heart went all thuddy. Doing favours for bad

people can only end badly. Just ask Guido Giuilani from *Mafia Saga*. I asked Marshall what this favour was.

He shoved the flowers into my hands and said, 'You need to take these to my girlfriend.'

I looked down at the flowers then back at his face. His jaw clenched. I asked him who his girlfriend was. He tutted and jabbed me with his finger. 'Don't you know nothing? She's Sheridan O'Neill in Year Nine. Make sure you tell her they're from Marshall, or I'll pound you.'

'But how will I know who she is?' I said to him.

He went, 'ASK AROUND,' and shoved me up the road.

Why did I have to leave the school? Why was I that bothered about chocolate? I went through what I had to do. I figured I would find Kirsty and Ash, ask them who this Sheridan O'Neill was and give her the flowers. It would be just like Eugene Smythe in *Codebreakers 3*, when he had to hand the secret files to Agent Florence Barkley. I had fifteen minutes to get all that done so I sped up.

I sensed a car slowing down and pulling up alongside me. I didn't look. They were probably going to ask me for directions and I hadn't a clue where anything was. I might as well have been on Pluto.

'Stop where you are.'

Oh God, what now? I turned around and saw it. A police car. The officer got out and approached me. He was huge, but not like Marshall Cremaine huge, more, I-have-eaten-every-pie-in-the-country-and-I'm-still-hungry huge.

He nodded at me and said, 'They're some lovely flowers you have there, who are they for?'

I started to panic again and I went, 'Um, Sheridan?'

He said, 'You don't sound like you're from round here, son.'

I babbled something about being from the Midlands and it being my first day in school and he chuckled in this proper patronizing way and said, 'I don't think shoplifting is a good way to ingratiate yourself at your new school, do you?'

I was like, 'Wha? Shoplifting?'

He laughed again and said, 'We've just had a report of a bunch of flowers, very much like the ones you're carrying, being stolen from Johnson's shop up the road. Now, are you going to explain to me what happened?'

I couldn't believe it. That knuckle-dragging idiot stole those flowers, then made me take them to his girlfriend. I tried to explain what happened, but it came out as a load of blah blah blah. I wouldn't have believed me if I were him.

'All right, in the car,' he said.

Yep, my first day at school and I was in the back of a police car. Amazing. I started going through how I was going to explain all this to Dad. It would surely make him have a full-blown nervous breakdown.

We pulled up outside the shop and the copper made me

go inside. He went up to the owners, pointed at me and said, 'This him?'

The woman shook her head and was like, 'Nah, it was a big lad. He's not big.'

The bloke agreed, saying, 'The lad that nicked the flowers was three times bigger than him.'

I was like, OK, I get it. I'm small.

Anyway, this meant that the policeman accepted my explanation and let me go, saying he was going off to find this Marshall Cremaine.

When I got back, I told Kirsty and Ash what happened. After about ten minutes of 'No way, you're lying, NO WAAAAYYY,' Kirsty said, 'I'm glad they assigned you to us now, Nelson. I can already tell a lot of weird stuff is going to happen to you.'

I met Mary at the bus stop after school and she'd already made a best friend for life—this little lad called Oscar with a blackcurrant moustache and an  eye patch. I think Mary liked him because he reminded her of Peter the Pirate. She asked me if I thought Oscar could come to our house and play one day. I said I doubted it because we lived too far away. I didn't say that it was because our house was a death trap and Dad would probably make him build a shed or something like that.

WHAT'S THE MATTER, BOY?

We started getting into a bit of a routine for the next couple of days. Dad fixed the hot water and electric lights, so we weren't having to rely on kettles and candles and the place was starting to seem a little more normal. I mean, there was still no TV or computers, but Dad did allow us a wind-up radio. Unfortunately, being out in the sticks, the only channels we could get were Morris Dancing FM and the frequencies from Scarfwick's transmitter, which were really too rude to be broadcast pre-watershed.

None of this was getting Mum back, though. Mary kept asking Dad where she was. Dad wouldn't answer her.

I wanted to continue with my video plan, but I couldn't get access to a computer at all. There were only three PCs in the library at school, and they were always being used. The only hope I had of getting on one was at after-school club, and that wasn't even an option because I had to get the bus home with Mary.

As well as not being able to do anything about Mum, this also meant that I had no way of researching anything for homework. One day, Mr Tronk asked me to stay behind after English class.

He said, 'Well, partner, I been reading your homework, and I can tell you ain't no dummy. Your spelling is perfect. Your presentation is grade A. Problem is, I don't think you did your research.'

I asked what he meant, trying to sound casual. He took off his shades and replaced them with a sensible pair of reading glasses. 'Just looky here,' he jabbed my exercise book. '"Doing plays was difficult in Shakespeare's time because marauding gangs of Vikings would often disrupt the performances. That was if the Ancient Romans couldn't stop them."'

He looked at me and raised an eyebrow.

I said, 'Is that not right, then?'

He lowered his eyebrow and swivelled around to face me. 'What's the matter, boy? You prefer using your imagination to researching facts? 'Cause that's a good thing when you're writing stories, but the rest of the time, it's gonna be a problem.'

I was about to tell him. How my dad won't allow computers and how I don't live within twenty miles of a library. But then I wondered what would happen if I did. Would Dad get in trouble? Was he breaking the law by doing what he was doing? Would we get taken away and put in some kind of home? As bad as Dad was, I didn't

remembered seeing that brook on the way in on my first day. The water is covered by a thick layer of green gunk. I swear, if you fall into that, you'll come out radioactive.

Marshall grabbed my arm in a vice-grip. I struggled, but the other three manhandled me so I couldn't get away.

Kirsty said, 'That's it, I'm telling,' but one of the goons stopped her with his massive arm.

I didn't know what to do. I knew there was no way I could go in that brook.

I examined my enemies, analyzing them for weaknesses like you do in *Exoskeleton War*. Head: No Weakness. Torso: No Weakness. Legs: No Weakness.

Damn. These were tough exoskeletons. Then a siren sounded in my brain.

POSSIBLE VULNERABILITY DETECTED— MENTAL CAPACITY.

That was when it hit me—I could exploit the fact that they obviously weren't very clever. But how? Well, I was new. No one knew anything about me. I could be whatever I wanted to be. In a weird way, it was kind of like the online gaming community.

'IF YOU DON'T UNHAND ME IMMEDIATELY, I WILL BE FORCED TO ENGAGE YOU IN COMBAT,' I yelled.

They did not unhand me. They just laughed. Really hard.

I said, 'I'M SERIOUS. I AM TRAINED IN THE WAYS OF THE SAMURAI.'

They laughed again, and Marshall said, 'All right, lads, let him go. I want to be engaged in combat.'

They finally 'unhanded' me and I shook myself down like a boxer. I thought back to *Kung Fu Warrior*, a game based on all those old martial arts movies my dad used to watch before he went insane.

Marshall was like, 'Come on then, let's see it.'

I took a deep breath and did this karate stance like that Bruce Lee bloke. I tried to hide the fact that I only ever went to one karate lesson and didn't even make it all the way through because I accidentally kicked myself in the face.

'I summon the power of the lotus dragon,' I said. 'Prepare to suffer.'

I swear, I sounded proper hard. I felt like wobbling my mouth around a bit so it looked like I was badly dubbed, but I decided against it.

The bullies laughed again, but not so loud. I had to ramp it up a bit.

I went, 'HWWWAAAAAAAAA YOOOOOOWWWWWW!' and started windmilling my arms and legs around like a confused daddy longlegs.

They all stepped back.

'AYAYAYAYAYAYCHAAAAA!'

Marshall was trying to play it cool, but I could tell I was freaking him out. I could see it in his eyes. He said,

'He's mad lads, let's leave him, yeah? Don't want to catch it.' Then they turned and walked away. Fast.

I know some of you are going to write, 'Yeah, whatevs, jog on,' in the comments, but I swear, that was exactly how it happened. Word soon spread across school that I was a tough guy not to be messed with, and Marshall forgot about the flowers.

After that, Kirsty and Ash started involving me in everything—making me the official third member of their group. I thought it might have been because I could scare bullies away, or maybe because of my dynamite personality. Kirsty soon put me right on that score.

'It's because you're a nutter,' she said. 'I've always wanted to be mates with the school nutter.'

Well, it's nice to feel wanted.

One day, they were asking me about home and everything and they said that they would come out to visit me one day, and I must have seemed really worried about it, because then they basically made me tell them everything. And I mean everything. I didn't want to, but it all came gushing out, like when you bomb another town's flood defences in *Apocalypse Wars III*.

'So you're saying you need some money in order to get your mum back, so you can move back to a normal house?' Kirsty said to me, her eyes going all massive behind her glasses like they always do when she's up to something.

'Pretty much, yeah,' I said to her.

She turned and whacked Ash on the shoulder and said, 'Did you hear that? We HAVE to help now, it's basically our duty.'

Ash looked up from his Superman comic and said, 'Oh God, what are you planning now?'

Kirsty stared into the distance and gripped the tip of her tongue between her teeth. After a few seconds, she said, 'I don't know yet. But I'll think of something. Trust me.'

Ash sighed and said, 'You know, before you arrived, it had been exactly seven months since her last stupid scheme. Seven glorious months.'

TONS

A couple of days later, I was sitting in the lunch hall, staring at this other kid's backpack. It was a *League of Ninjas* design. What I would have given to have been able to play that sweet, sweet game for two minutes. To perform just one stealthy take-down. It would have been the stuff of magic.

I shook my head to try and snap myself out of it. How could I be daydreaming about games when my mum was missing? Dad was only getting worse, too. His beard was growing longer by the day, and he was working on a life-size wooden model of Panther Blimmington-Weltby. Imagine being the tree that had to be cut down to make a Panther Blimmington-Weltby. I think I'd rather be toilet paper. I felt a jab in my ribs.

'OK, OK,' Kirsty said. 'We've put our heads together and we've had an idea to make you some cash. A proper idea.'

Ash gave me a look as if to say, 'I actually had nothing to do with this.' Can't blame him for distancing himself. Kirsty's previous genius idea had been to stand outside the shop and get an adult to buy me a lottery ticket. When I'd finally plucked up the courage to ask someone, he'd taken the money out of my hand, got back in his car, and driven off.

I said to her, 'Really? What is it?'

She was like, 'That is top secret until we arrive at the location—can't risk anyone overhearing and tipping off the feds.'

'The feds?' I said. 'What are you—'

Kirsty smashed her index finger against my lips. 'Shhhh. They have eyes and ears everywhere.'

I glanced at Ash but he just shrugged.

She said, 'Meet us at the bus stop tomorrow at five. Then, all will be revealed.'

I prised her finger away from my mouth. 'I don't know if I can do that, Dad gets a bit weird about me going out.'

She was having none of it. She said, 'Tell him you have to come to mine to work on a project. Tell him it's about nature or some crap, he's bound to love that.'

I said maybe.

She poked my shoulder with her super sharp finger of doom. 'Maybe nothing. This has the potential to bag us tons of money. Do you hear me, Nelson? TONS.'

'All right, all right, I'll be there,' I said.

THE CAR PARK SCAM

The next afternoon, I took the bus to Snessport. It felt odd being on it at the weekend. I gave Dad the nature homework excuse and as Kirsty predicted, he ate it up. The fact that she was right about something made me feel ever so slightly better about what was about to happen. Still, my mind was racing. 'Tons of money,' she said. Were we going to rob a bank? Because even though I completed *The Heist* in under two days, I didn't think I could do it for real.

Ash and Kirsty were waiting for me at the bus stop. Kirsty was hopping from foot to foot. I asked her if she would actually tell me what the plan was. She grabbed me by the shoulders, pulled me in close and whispered, 'We're doing the car park scam.'

I was like, 'Is that supposed to mean something to me?'

Kirsty chuckled, lightly slapped my cheek, and said, 'You will see, my son.'

We headed up the street past school, then turned down Hangman's Road. I know, creepy name. It's a long, single-track country lane that leads to Flendon Country Park. We kept going until we arrived at a big, creaky gate. Kirsty pushed it open. Behind it was a field, fenced in on all sides.

I was stumped. What was the plan? Plant some seeds and hope a money tree grows? I demanded they spill.

Kirsty giggled and was all, 'Tell him, Ash, tell him!'

Ash rolled his eyes and said, 'Basically, the circus is on up the road. And the parking there is a rip.'

'A TOTAL rip,' said Kirsty as she pulled a wooden plank out of her backpack. 'Eight quid!'

Ash told me that Kirsty had the idea to open this field and charge people a fiver to park there.

Kirsty turned the plank around to reveal PARKING £5 scrawled across it in red paint.

I was like, 'Hmm, doesn't this land belong to somebody?'

Kirsty blew a raspberry and said, 'This is land. You can't own land.'

I said, 'Actually, I'm pretty sure you can.'

She was like, 'Look, do you want money for your mummy or not?'

I said I did.

She said, 'Well then, stop being a wuss and help me put up some more of these signs.'

I did as I was told. I glanced around the field and tried to size it up. Applying the parking principles from the carjacking missions in *Streets of Chicago III*, I estimated that we would get fifty vehicles into the field. At a fiver each, that was two hundred and fifty quid. Not bad for an afternoon's work.

The first cars soon began to arrive. Kirsty took their money and me and Ash guided them into the spaces. Within an hour, we were nearly full. Loads of people were really happy about saving three quid. Kirsty grinned at me and gave me a quick flash of the cash. It felt good— we were making money by providing a service the public wanted.

When the traffic had quietened down, we sat on a fence at the end of the field and watched the sun go down. Thinking about it, I don't think I'd ever watched a real sunset before. I'd seen plenty of pretend ones on *Vampire Hunters*, because that's when all the bad guys come out.

It made me think about Mum. Maybe she was somewhere, watching the same sunset. I held my share of the cash in my hand. I was another step closer to getting her back, I just knew it.

'Oi!' A shout echoed across the field. 'What do you think you're doing?'

'Oh. Cack,' said Kirsty.

I turned around and saw the farmer storming towards us. I went to run but then I saw the shotgun slung across his back. He would definitely take me down—just like Wild Zeke in *Crazy Rednecks 2: Hillbilly's Revenge*.

I held up my hands and squeaked, 'Don't shoot.'

He barked at us, 'Off my fence—NOW!'

We did as we were told.

'What do you think gives you the right to let people park in my field?'

Ash said, 'What do you know? Looks like you can own land.'

Kirsty was all, 'Blah, blah, blah.'

The farmer yelled, 'ANSWER ME.'

Kirsty tutted. 'All right, tired.' She turned around and rubbed her eyes so they went all watery. When she looked back at him, she was making a screwed-up sad face.

'I'm so sowwy,' she went. 'We didn't know we were doing anything wrong. We're only kids.'

She was actually pretending to cry. I swear to God, guys, she is an evil genius.

I could tell the farmer didn't know what to do. He said, 'I've just planted these fields. I'm going to have to do it again now. Do you have any idea how much that is going to cost me?'

I gulped and said, 'We really are sorry. Please, take our money.'

Kirsty immediately stopped crying and kicked me in the shin.

Luckily Ash agreed with me, and told Kirsty to give up the money. She agreed. Eventually.

So we walked away from the car park scam with no money at all. Kirsty was NOT happy. She was like, 'Ugh, I can't believe it. If we'd left just a couple of minutes earlier instead of staying to watch that poxy sunset, we'd have been away. Stupid nature.'

Stupid nature? Imagine if Dad heard her say that.

She wouldn't let it go, even as we headed back to the bus stop. She kept telling me and Ash off for giving up the money so easily.

I said, 'He did have a gun.'

'Whatever,' she shot back. 'This scam could not have gone any worse.'

HONK HONK.

'There they are, get them!'

What. The. Hell.

We spun around and saw them. A massive horde striding down the lane towards us. There were a couple of clowns, an acrobat or two, a strongman, and I'm sure I spotted a bearded lady. Someone must have tipped them off that we were responsible for their drop in profits.

'CIRCUS PEOPLE!' Ash yelled. 'RUN!'

We belted down the lane away from the motley gang of weirdoes.

'Why didn't you consider this?' I panted at Kirsty as we ran. 'Didn't you think they would notice?'

'No,' she shouted back. 'I thought we'd get away with it because clowns are stupid.'

'Hey, I heard that,' one of them yelled.

We came out of Hangman's Road and back onto the High Street. It was deserted. Still even if it wasn't, who would be able to stop a gang of marauding circus freaks? My heart pumped and my temples throbbed. I thought I was going to die. When people say how they want to go, it's always in bed, surrounded by their family. Not clubbed to death by an angry dwarf outside the Londis.

That was when I saw it: our only hope. The bus. I pumped my legs faster and waved at the driver. The horde of circus people screamed at us to stop, but we couldn't. We didn't have any money to give them. I dived onto the bus. When the driver saw what was coming, he looked like he was going to have a heart attack. He started pulling away. Kirsty managed to jump on but Ash was still stranded. I shouted for the driver to stop but he wouldn't. He had gone proper pale. He must have been one of those people who are scared of clowns.

I leaned out and held my hand out to Ash. He grabbed it and I pulled him aboard, just before the doors closed.

As I sat down and tried desperately to get my breath back, I made a promise to myself never to ask them for help ever again.

NATURE'S CARVERY

The three of us were a bit depressed the following Monday at school. Kirsty seemed to think I was a jinx, saying stuff like, 'I've never had two money-making schemes in a row fail. I think you have bad ju-ju, Nelson.'

After school, Dad sat Mary and I down at the kitchen table. He had this mad look in his eyes. Even madder than usual. His beard was now taking up occupied territory around his neck and he appeared to be wearing a shirt he had made himself out of tea towels and bits of old sack.

Mary bounced in her seat and asked what was for dinner. She'd been feeling better since I told her I was trying to get Mum back. She was even getting into trouble at her new school. Her teacher found me at the gates and told me that Mary had been caught teaching the entire class Scarfwick's rude word.

Now, I know she's five and it's wrong, but it was really hard to keep a straight face. I made Mary promise never to say it again, and quietly slipped the letter to Dad out of the window of the bus when we were thirty miles from home.

She totally idolized this Oscar kid. She even wanted

an eye patch so she could look like him. This once, she turned around to me and said, 'Nelson, what's assmar?'

I told her it sounds like another one of Scarfwick's naughty words and she should never repeat it, but she said, 'No, assmar. Oscar says he's got assmar and I want it.'

I finally twigged. 'Oh, asthma? Yeah, you don't want that.'

Mary scowled and folded her arms. 'Why not?'

I said, 'Because it makes you get out of breath really quick and you cough loads and you have to suck medicine out of an inhaler.'

This wasn't doing the job, though. She was like, 'But Oscar gets out of doing PE 'cause of his assmar. Today he started breathing funny so he didn't have to do running and after he told me that he was making it up. When I tried it, the teacher told me off because I haven't got assmar, and I had to run. I hate running. When I grow up, I want assmar.'

She's weird.

Anyway, back to the table. Dad told Mary that we didn't have any dinner. This was not good news. My stomach was grumbling up a storm. I briefly considered hot-wiring his car and finding the nearest Maccy's drive-through.

He leaned forward and whispered, 'Tonight, my children, we are going to find our own dinner.' He stood up, pointed at the window, and said, 'We will forage. We will find our food in nature. We will hunt, gather, and feast upon its bounty.'

My head slowly sunk into my hands. This is how Panther Blimmington-Weltby lives. We were doing everything like him. Before I knew it, we would be in the Arctic Circle, eating seals, and fighting polar bears.

I suggested that we just went for a carvery. After all, it's easier and doesn't involve killing things.

Dad slid a home-made slingshot across the table.

'Out there, Nelson,' he said, 'is nature's carvery.'

Seriously guys, if you've ever heard a more mental sentence than that, stick it in the comments because I want to hear it.

I was going to just point-blank refuse to do it and 'forage' something from the cupboards. No such luck. We really were out of everything. Plus, the only shop in Sheepy Murva sold fishing tackle, and I wasn't desperate enough to eat maggots. Yet.

I picked up my slingshot and headed out. Dad was taking Mary into the woods on the hill behind our house while I had to stay in the area off the dirt track. Mary tried to fake 'assmar' to get out of it but Dad was having none of it.

I knew there was no way I was going to shoot anything with that. I won't even step on a spider. I'm strictly a glass-

and-paper kind of guy, and I doubt they make glasses big enough for pheasants. Yes, I know I'm probably going to be down-voted for that and called a wimp, but it's just the way I am.

I thought my best hope might be to find some fruit and berries. Dad could worry about killing stuff if he was so bothered.

I crept through the thick bushes and trees at the end of our front garden. There were berries everywhere but I had no idea if they were edible. Of course, this was exactly the kind of thing I'd be able to research on the INTERNET. Ugh. It was getting darker and colder and rain started falling. It was proper miserable.

I had to find something and fast. This was nothing like that PC game, *Frontier World*, where there were always deer and rabbits and buffalo and loads of useful plants and herbs. There was nothing. We were going to have to eat twigs. Or so I thought.

I stumbled through the bushes, the thorns scratching my skin, getting more lost and confused with every step, until I came to a clearing. I couldn't believe my eyes. There were vegetables growing everywhere—carrots, cauliflowers, potatoes, all in neat rows. I thought it must have been that nature's bounty thing Dad had been blabbering on about.

I started scooping up all I could carry. We really were

73

going to have a proper feast. I pulled the bottom of my coat out, creating a big pouch I could pile the veg into. Dad was going to be so happy with my foraging.

Before I could head back to the house, a bright light engulfed my face and I was blinded. I heard a voice.

It said, 'HEY, WHAT ARE YOU DOING?'

A PRETTY IMPRESSIVE LIE

The next thing I knew, I was sitting in a chair in Primrose's living room. Even though I was scared, I still noticed how different it was to ours. The walls were all plastered and painted in nice colours. There were paintings up. Her floor was varnished bare wood with thick rugs on it. She even had a TV. I know it sounds weird, but I felt like hugging it.

Primrose came out of the kitchen carrying two cups of tea. She handed me one and sat down on the sofa opposite. Her face looked grim.

She told me I had two choices: tell her why I was stealing from her allotment or tell the police. My palms started to sweat. The first time I ended up in a police car was a misunderstanding, this time they would have me bang to rights.

I took a deep breath and told her. I told her everything. About how Mum had left and Dad had gone crazy and made us live like something out of *The Jungle Book*. I didn't mean to, but it all just came out.

When I finally stopped talking, Primrose still had that

grim look on her face, but her eyes were glistening. She said, 'You poor little things. Do you want me to talk to your father?'

I took a sip of my tea. It was still scalding hot and burned my mouth. I said, 'That wouldn't be a good idea. He said we're not supposed to talk to you.'

She asked why.

I said, 'It's because you're a web designer and he thinks the internet is the cause of all the evil in the world.'

She was like, 'But that's ridiculous. How can you survive without it in this day and age? I mean, how do you do homework?'

I shrugged, not really knowing what to say.

Primrose put her tea down and went into another room. She came back in holding a laptop. My eyes nearly zoomed out of my head. She said it was for me. I tried to refuse, but she insisted. She had just upgraded to a newer model—this sleek looking thing sitting on the table.

She made me promise to keep it hidden. I nodded so hard, I thought my head was going to drop off.

She asked me if I had any contact details for my mum at all, but I didn't. Primrose fired up her new laptop and sat next to me. She really wanted to help me find Mum. I'm guessing she was picking up on a strong vibe that my dad was going a bit cuckoo. Well, she said, 'He's not in a good place,' which basically means the same thing, doesn't it?

Anyway, after Googling, scouring social networks, message boards, local news, you name it, Primrose came up with nothing. She told me to leave it with her and that she was going to make it her own special little project. When she closed the window, I caught a glimpse of the one behind it. It was a half-finished website for a computer games shop. A surge of excitement shot through my body and I must have made some kind of eager noise, because she turned and looked at me.

'You like games, I guess?' she said.

I was like, 'Yeah, a little bit.' Ha ha HAAA!

She said, 'Must be hard not being able to play any more.'

I shrugged and tried to make it seem like it wasn't the hardest thing ever and that my bones weren't literally aching to hold a controller.

'Well see if you can help me with this,' she said. 'I know nothing about computer games.'

She pointed at this sidebar in the adventure games section. 'I need something here.'

I racked my brains and thought of all the best adventure games of recent years, then I did a quick image search and showed her pictures of the main characters. She told me they would look great as a collage and thanked me for my help. She even told me I had a real talent for web design. I'm sure she was just being nice, but even so, it made me feel good.

Before I left, Primrose went into the kitchen and came back with a big bag full of food. She put the laptop in along with a piece of paper with her Wi-Fi login details on.

She told me that if I ever needed anything, I only had to ask and not nick it out of her allotment. I thanked her loads and ran back up the drive. It was pitch black. I quickly ducked into one of the outbuildings and hid the laptop behind a stack of wood leaning against the wall.

When I went back into the house, Dad was doing his nut, like, 'Where have you been? I've been looking everywhere for you!'

I lifted up my bag and said, 'Been foraging.'

Dad was amazed. All his and Mary's foraging had turned up was a handful of blackberries and an old fish tank that Mary was going to use to make a worm farm.

I emptied the sack onto the table. Dad said he was impressed with my foraging skills but wanted to know how I found tins of baked beans and a box of chocolate fingers.

Ah. I probably should have checked that this stuff was forageable. I said, 'Oh, there was a boat in the harbour. They had to get rid of their stuff because they were going to sink.'

You have to admit, guys, that was a pretty impressive lie.

GERTRUDE

I was super excited at school the next day. I was planning on getting my YouTube channel back up and running. I decided to broach the subject with Ash and Kirsty. Kirsty agreed it sounded like a grand money-making scheme. Through a mouthful of sandwich, she told me that her favourite vlogger was Midlake Darston, mainly because he was 'soooooooo cute'.

I asked her what he talked about.

She shook her head and swallowed. 'Talk? I have no idea what he says. I just stare at his eyes and his cheekbones and his dimples and his oooohhh . . .'

'So you're saying you have to be good-looking to be a YouTube person?'

This time, Ash chipped in. 'God, no. The only YouTuber I watch is this bloke called Roger Piney—he talks about Superman comics.'

'Now there's a surprise,' said Kirsty.

Ash laughed proper sarcastically—like you could hear the individual 'ha's'. He said, 'Roger is cross-eyed and has a uni-brow and wears knitted tanktops, and he gets loads of views.'

Kirsty was like, 'Wow, he sounds DREAMY. Anyway, what are your videos going to be about, Nels? How to do fake karate moves?'

My eyes darted to where Marshall and his gang of gorillas were sitting. I said, 'Shh, they don't know they're fake.'

Kirsty did a 'my lips are zipped' gesture. Ash said, 'Come on, tell us. Because if it's Batman, I'm not sure we can be friends any more.'

I was like, 'Well, I was thinking about talking about computer games, but I can't do that now.'

Kirsty said, 'Maybe you could do a video about punking circus people? I would totally watch that.'

I kept thinking about it all day. What could I talk about? What did I know about more than most people?

When Mary and I got home, the long grass and weeds out the front had been hacked away and replaced with an actual allotment and a chicken coop with one hen.

'OOOOOH, CHICKY CHICKY!' Mary squealed when she saw it.

Dad walked towards us, sweat running down his face into his beard. He said, 'Please don't infantilize the hen, Mary. She works for us.'

My eyes bulged and I was like, 'You mean that chicken made that allotment?'

Dad wiped the sweat from his forehead with a filthy rag and looked at me like I was a massive idiot. He said, 'No, she will provide us with eggs. And eventually when the time is right . . .' He made a thumbs-down gesture. Luckily, Mary didn't see that because she was too busy petting the chicken.

She was going, 'I'm going to call you Gertrude, like Peter the Pirate's parrot.' She picked it up then threw it outwards and yelled, 'Get 'em, Gertrude!' You know, like Peter the Pirate does. When Mary did it to the chicken, though, all it did was flap its wings a couple of times, then land on the floor and peck at some grain.

I told Mary that naming the hen was probably a bad idea and took her inside. Once she'd quietened down about wanting to play with Gertrude, I went back out to Dad. He was planting turnips and saying, 'Ah, I see you've come to observe our latest step towards self-sufficiency.'

I said, 'Yeah, something like that. Actually, I wanted to talk to you about the outhouse.'

He stopped digging and leaned on his spade. 'Remember what I told you, son. If it's yellow, let it mellow. If it's brown, flush it down.'

Ugh. I said, 'No, not that outhouse. The other one. I was thinking I could use it.'

Dad ran a hand through his beard and asked me what I wanted the other outhouse for.

I was like, 'Umm, a place to do homework. A place to think. A place to . . .' I stopped and thought of what he would say. 'A place to be at one with nature.'

Dad's face broke out into this massive proud grin. He said, 'That sounds like an excellent idea. Do you need a hand clearing it out?'

I yelled, 'NO!' a bit too loud, then said, 'I mean, no, I want to do it myself. After all, it is my Fortress of Solitude.'

Dad looked confused. I'd obviously been hanging around with Ash too much.

I headed in there with the lamp from my bedroom. I placed the laptop on the old workbench. There was a grubby double electrical socket in there. I plugged in the lamp and switched it on. It didn't blow me through the roof so it must have been OK.

I could hear Dad digging and Mary playing outside. I felt bad keeping this from them but it was the only way.

I turned on the laptop. It was a really great model. A lot better than my old one. I said a quiet thank you to Primrose and got on with what I needed to do.

First, I quickly did my homework research, then headed to the Lugs YouTube channel. That video I made about TechOps now had a grand total of seventeen views and one comment. Which was

U SUCK.

Reply · 👍 👎

I sat there, staring at the crumbling wall, the smell of mould getting up my nose. What was I going to talk about, anyway? I remembered what Kirsty said about Midlake Darston. He was super popular. If I could talk about the same kind of things as him, I could be, too. Even if I didn't have swoony cheekbones and dreamy eyes and blah, blah, blah.

I clicked onto his channel. Six million subscribers. Oh my God. I thought this guy must have been a genius to get a following that big. As I watched his latest video, I started to change that opinion slightly. Now, Midlake, if you're watching this, and that is unlikely, because you're probably sitting around the pool being fanned by a load of bikini models, but if you are, I don't mean to offend you, but come on. The video I watched was just him talking about how he'd been to the shops to buy a pair of trainers. It had nine hundred thousand views and three thousand likes and the comments below were all

I LOVE YOU SO MUCH, MIDLAKE. NOTICE ME!!!! AAAARRRRGGHH!

Reply · 👍 👎

And all he was doing was talking about his life. I could do that. Easy. With all the stuff I had been going through, I had loads to talk about. And it was actually kind of interesting.

I pressed record on the webcam and I just talked. About how Mum had gone and I'd moved to the middle of nowhere with no computer games and that we were having to forage for our dinners. The main message I wanted to get across was that kids should appreciate their nice clean homes with central heating and TVs and toilets that were inside and didn't give your bum frostbite.

I stopped talking and pressed upload. I didn't watch it back. I thought it would be better if it was unedited. More emotional, like.

As I watched it being sent out into the world, I got the same feeling I had when I wrote that bottle message. Like I was reaching out from the wilderness. That somehow, Mum would see it and come back.

Well, if YouTube could change the life of Midlake Darston, then why not me?

STOP WHINING, YOU WUSS

Mr Tronk seemed to be impressed with my improved homework. He gave me 'four hound dogs out of five'. Whatever that meant. At lunch time, me, Ash, and Kirsty settled into our Fortress of Solitude with a can of Coke between us. They asked me if I'd made my video yet. I was like, 'Hmm, maybe.'

Kirsty was all, 'Ah, brilliant, let's see it!'

I said, 'Ohhh, you could, but the library is always too busy at lunch time. What a shame.'

Kirsty looked at me as if I'd just floated down from my zeppelin, using an umbrella as a parachute. She took her phone out and waved it around, like, 'Um, hello? Never heard of one of these?'

Ugh. I think I drooled a little bit.

She pressed the YouTube app and asked the name of my channel. I looked at the floor and passed Ash the can. 'Not telling you.'

Kirsty shoved my shoulder and said, 'Come on, how do you expect to become a YouTube star if no one watches your videos?'

Hmm. I suppose she had a point. I said, 'Fine. It's Lugs.'

Ash looked at me weird and asked me why I picked that name. Without looking up, Kirsty flicked my ear with her spare hand and said, 'Do you really need to ask that question? Ah, here we go. *My Life in the Wild.*'

She looked up at me and raised her eyebrows. 'The wild? Bit dramatic. Makes you sound like you were raised by wolves.'

'That would explain the smell,' said Ash.

I socked him on the arm, making Coke fly up his nose.

They gathered around and watched my video. I had to stick my fingers in my ears. Why is it the voice we hear in our heads is nothing like the one everyone else hears?

Anyway, Kirsty and Ash really liked it. Kirsty said she was going to share it on her Facebook. I tried to stop her but it was already done. Ah well, I suppose being shared is the best way to go viral.

The next day, a couple of Year Nines heckled me outside the science labs. All, 'Hey, it's the wild boy!' Then some other lad stopped me and pointed at a lightbulb, going, 'Oooh. Light. Indoor light. MAAAAGIIIICCC!'

I took up a karate stance. He ran away.

That night, I sneaked into the outhouse and checked the stats. One hundred views and one comment. It said,

Well, it was an improvement, but it wasn't going to make me enough money to get Mum back. I realized that it's all very well just talking about living wild, but maybe viewers had to see it. I thought back to Panther Blimmington-Weltby. He got famous from showing TV viewers how to use nature to survive. Maybe that could be my thing. I could be a young, internet version.

The first problem was my name. Nelson doesn't exactly make you think of wild-living and self-sufficiency. I needed an animal name like Panther. I considered all the big cats.

Leopard? Sounds too much like Leonard.

Cheetah? Sounds too much like cheater.

Lion? Sounds too much like lying.

Cougar? Ah, now there was a good one. Cougar Lambsley. That sounded like a tough, wild name. That's what my videos would be called from now on. *Cougar Lambsley's Living in the Wild*.

The only problem I had then was how to film it. Lugging the laptop about outside was asking for trouble. I needed a small camera that could easily be hidden.

After dinner (vegetable stew, probably) I told Dad I was heading for the outhouse, but then sneaked behind it, through the bushes and to the only person who would be able to help me.

And I don't mean Scarfwick.

Q

Primrose seemed proper happy to see me and offered me a cup of tea. I didn't really fancy one, but I liked sitting in her living room so I agreed. It was nice to be in a normal house for a while.

She passed me the cup of tea with a worried look on her face and said, 'Now I don't want you to take this the wrong way, but your mum's not a missing person, is she?'

I was like, 'No, she left us a note. She just didn't say where she went. Or why.'

Primrose clutched her mug and blew the hot tea. She said, 'I just haven't been able to find any trace of her, darling.'

I slumped in my seat a little.

She said, 'That's not to say we won't find her. It might just be a little tricky. Anyway, to what do I owe this pleasure?'

My legs started shaking. I tried to stop them, but the more I thought about it, the worse it got. I swear, at one point, it was so bad, I almost vibrated out of the room on the sofa.

I was all, 'Um, well, the thing is,' about it, but eventually, I managed to blurt out that I had to make a video for homework and, 'Could I please borrow a camera if you have one if it's not too much trouble, please, thank you.'

When I looked up, Primrose had narrowed her eyes at me. It was just like a look Mum used to give me. As if she could tell I was lying. What gave me away? Ah, it was probably my jittery feet tap-dancing on the wooden floor. She asked me what I really needed it for.

I took a deep breath and told her about my YouTube plan. It felt so stupid, hearing it out loud. She did laugh a little bit, too and was all, 'Well, it can't hurt,' and 'Stranger things have happened.'

Anyway, after I'd promised that I wasn't going to use it to film something illegal, she agreed to let me borrow one. She said she felt like Q from off James Bond. The camera was small enough to fit in the palm of my hand. More importantly, it was small enough to hide.

Before she handed it over, she stopped and asked, 'Do you really think money will bring your mum back?'

I thought about it. It had to be the reason she left. I mean, it's what they were always arguing about. Plus, maybe if I got YouTube famous enough, Mum would see my videos and be horrified at how Dad was making us live and come back to save us. I mean, she did still love us. I'm sure she did.

When I left Primrose's house, with the camera in my hand, I felt kind of sad. I liked just sitting in her living room and talking to her. In a weird way, it was kind of like having a mum again.

SECRET MISSION

The next morning, we sat down to a delicious Saturday breakfast of scrambled eggs.

'These are from Gertrude,' Mary said to me.

I nodded, my mouth full.

'They came out of her BOTTOM,' she said.

I pushed my plate away. I mean, I knew that all along but hearing it in actual words was too much.

As I was getting up, Dad brought the post in. He had a smile on his big, hairy face and was all, 'Ah, my first whittling orders. Finally, my hard work is paying off.'

Then he dropped an envelope in front of me and raised an eyebrow. 'A letter for you, son.'

My heart raced. Mum had found out where we lived and was writing to tell us that she was coming home.

I tore open the envelope.

Dear Nelson,

Your letter washed up in Hunstanton. I ain't your mum but if my kid was as big a wimp as you, I'd run away too.

P.S. Nelson is a daft name.

I couldn't believe it. I had to be the first person in history to be trolled by mail.

Dad asked what it was. I told him it was an invite to a school trip to an internet museum. Nice save.

After breakfast, I headed to the outhouse to fetch my equipment. The night before, I had dug a little hole under the workbench, lined it with canvas, and put the laptop and camera in there. Then I covered them in straw and another layer of canvas. It was proper exciting. I felt like William Darcy in *Deep Undercover*.

As I left the outhouse, Mary was standing there, holding Gertrude under her arm.

'WhereareyougoingwhatareyoudoingcanIcome?' She bounced up and down and the chicken looked like it was going to puke.

'I'm just nipping out for a couple of hours,' I told her.

She grinned like mad and was like, 'We're coming with you!'

I said, 'Ummm, you can't.'

Her smile dissolved and her chin wobbled. She asked why.

I couldn't look at her. I said, 'Because I'm going on a secret mission.'

She was all, 'But I want to go on the secret mission!'

There was no way I could let Mary come. I mean, Panther Blimmington-Weltby didn't have a five-year-old girl helping him when he was sucking water out of a cactus in the desert, did he?

'You will,' I said. 'But you have to stay here and make sure Daddy doesn't come looking for me. If he does, we'll fail the mission.'

Mary's chin stopped wobbling. She said, 'So I'm important?'

I nodded and said, 'Very important.' I leaned down and whispered to her, 'The mission is to try and get Mummy back.'

She was like, 'Oh my gosh! Really?'

'Really.'

She grinned and saluted. 'Then we'd better not fail!'

She squeezed Gertrude and an egg dropped out. 'WOW!'

I headed into the woods. They were pretty thick close to the hill and I thought it would make a convincing forest.

When I found a particularly dark spot, I set up the camera on a tree stump. Here we go.

FULL OF THE JOYS OF NATURE

I got back to the house a couple of hours later. I was kind of banged up, but felt good about what I'd recorded.

Dad was sitting outside, whittling an elephant out of wood, wanting to know where I'd been all day.

I nervously touched the camera in my coat pocket and told him that I'd been enjoying nature, and was heading straight to the outhouse to note my observations in my journal.

He nodded approvingly and said something about how pleased he was that I was finally adjusting to our new way of life.

Mary and Gertrude came over. She winked at me. My sister, I mean, not the hen. She said, 'I kept an eye on Daddy. Mission complete.'

I gave her a sneaky thumbs up as I headed to the outhouse.

I started to download a free video-editing program. I had recorded quite a bit of footage and I was going to need something to splice it all together. While it was installing,

I logged onto YouTube. In the recommended bit were loads of videos by my favourite band, the Moonfaces. I clicked on the first clip—one of my favourite songs, 'Misery Guts'.

As the opening notes rang out, it was as if my ears had died and gone to heaven. I hadn't heard it in what felt like forever, and it made me realize how much stuff I was taking for granted in my old life: games, internet, games, music. Mum.

As 'Misery Guts' ended, and their next song 'Kick in the Face' started, I realized I had been crying. I wasn't sure for how long, but tears were rolling down my cheeks and onto the desk below. It got to the quiet bit of the song, before the chorus exploded back in, when I heard footsteps outside. Super fast, I slammed the laptop shut and dragged a load of school folders on top of it.

The door opened.

'What are you up to, son? I thought I heard noises.'

I quickly wiped my face. 'I was just singing while I worked. I am full of the joys of nature.'

Dad scoped the room out. I prayed that he didn't notice the cable trailing below the desk. He was like, 'OK. As long as you're having fun,' then turned and left. I felt bad about lying to Dad, but I figured that in the end he would understand because I was only doing it to get our family back together.

By the time this had happened, the editing software

had finished installing and I was ready to go. I plugged Primrose's camera into the laptop and started uploading all the clips I took. I watched the first one. It was too embarrassing to use.

I watched the second one. Same.

Then the third one.

Then the fourth.

Oh my God, why was I such a dork? I didn't look like a tough bushcraft guy. I looked like an idiot in a Kermit the Frog hoodie piddling around by some trees.

I desperately thought that maybe if I could sprinkle some editing magic over it that it would somehow appear better. It didn't.

ME: Hey guys, welcome to *Living in the Wild* with me, Cougar Lambsley. This is going to be your one-stop shop for everything you need to know about surviving in Mother Nature's unforgiving bosom.

QUICK EDIT HERE BECAUSE I LAUGH AT THE WORD 'BOSOM.'

ME: In this video, we will be focusing on bushcraft. First, I'll teach you how to build a shelter out of naturally occurring materials.

MUSIC COMES IN AND I'M EDITED TO WALK QUICKLY THROUGH THE WOODS. I LOOK SUPER

WEIRD. WHEN I FINALLY STOP, I'M NEXT TO A TREE WITH LOW BRANCHES.

ME: Right, all youdo is you snap some branches off a tree. Dead easy. Hmmm. Grrrrr. Break, you stupid . . . Ah. There we go. Now, I'll just snap off a few more.

AT THIS POINT I EDITED OUT THE NEXT TWENTY MINUTES OF ME BREAKING OFF TWIGS. WHAT CAN BE SEEN ON SCREEN IS A KIND OF PATHETIC PYRAMID MADE FROM THIN BRANCHES. TRUST ME, IT LOOKED BETTER IN THE FLESH.

ME: This is a solid structure that will withstand even the harshest of weather conditions.

I THEN LEAN ON IT AND IT COLLAPSES. CUT TO LATER WHEN IT'S REASSEMBLED. THIS TIME, I'M CAREFUL NOT TO TOUCH IT IN ANY WAY.

ME: OK, now I've made some adjustments, this shelter is a fortress that will resist gale force winds and pummelling rains.

I CRAWL INSIDE THE SHELTER. I'M ABOUT TO SAY HOW SECURE I FEEL WHEN SCARFWICK WALKS BY WITH HIS DOG, AHAB. AHAB THEN PROCEEDS TO WEE UP THE SIDE OF MY SHELTER, WHICH FIRES STRAIGHT THROUGH A GAP AND GOES IN MY HAIR. I JUMP TO MY FEET, WHICH SMASHES THE SHELTER INTO A MILLION PIECES.

SCARFWICK LAUGHS AND BARKS THE WORST, SECOND WORST, AND THIRD WORST SWEAR WORDS IN THE ENGLISH LANGUAGE.

THE VIDEO THEN CUTS TO ME STANDING IN FRONT OF A STREAM.

ME: When you're out in the wild, you have to eat. If you don't you are likely to starve to death, or at least go proper light-headed. Now, most people, when faced with an unforgiving forest miles away from the nearest Maccy's or Spar, would break down and give up. But not Cougar Lambsley. Cougar Lambsley does not know the meaning of the words 'give' and 'up'. Well, I do, I'm not an idiot, I'm just, like . . . super determined.

Anyway, I've come to this stream to catch some fish, and I'm not going to allow the small matter of me having no fishing equipment stop me getting my lunch. All you need to catch fish is one of these—a branch that has been sharpened to be all pointy. Then, when you see a fish, you stab it and pull it out of the water. In fact, look, there's one now. HAAAAIII YA! Got you!

No wait, that's not a fish. That does appear to be . . . a poo.

THE VIDEO CUTS TO ME STANDING BY A BUSH.

ME: If the fishing trip didn't go as well as you imagined—don't despair. Nature is like one big buffet, but know this: it is not all you can eat. Some foods are incredibly dangerous. Like this purple berry, for instance. Just one of these will make you vomit immediately. This red berry, though, is completely safe, and delicious.

I SMILE, PLUCK A RED BERRY FROM THE BUSH, AND POP IT INTO MY MOUTH. MY SMILE THEN BECOMES LESS CONVINCING, AND I DOUBLE OVER, PUKING EVERYWHERE.

THE VIDEO THEN CUTS TO ME, SITTING UP A TREE.

ME: I hope this video has been informative and that if you are ever in a wild situation, you can use the skills I have taught you. Thanks for watching *Living in the Wild* with me, Cougar Lambsley.

THE BRANCH SNAPS AND I FALL INTO A THORNY BUSH.

○

I buried my head in my hands. What a disaster. Why did I think I would make a convincing bushcrafter? I am no Panther Blimmington-Weltby. And why would I be? He's the son of an aristocrat who can afford to go around buying old houses and swanning around deserts and licking camel poo whenever he wants. I am the son of a mad bloke with a beard whose idea of a career is making giraffes out of bits of old tree.

The door opened again but I wasn't quick enough to cover up the laptop. I screwed my eyes shut and waited for the fury.

'What are you doing, Nelson? OH MY GOD, where did you get that puper?'

Yes, it was Mary. And yes, she does call computers 'pupers'. I don't know why.

I spun around and shut the door behind her.

'You cannot tell Daddy about this,' I said to her.

She was like, 'Why?'

I said, 'Because Daddy doesn't let us have pupers any more, does he? And if he finds out he'll be really angry.'

Mary bit her bottom lip. She said, 'But it's naughty to keep secrets from Daddy.'

I was like, 'I know, but this is part of our secret mission, OK? To get Mummy back?'

She still didn't look convinced. I had to try something else.

I said, 'Tell you what. If you promise not to tell Daddy, I'll let you watch *Peter the Pirate* on here.'

That did it, and after a pinky promise that she wouldn't squeal, I was standing guard outside while she watched two episodes back-to-back.

A couple of days later, I noticed a strange atmosphere at school. I could have sworn people were pointing at me and saying stuff like, 'I think that's him.'

To begin with I just thought I was being paranoid. But it started getting worse. A couple of people laughed when they saw me coming and made puking noises. This Year Eight cocked his leg up me and pretended to do a wee. I was beginning to wonder if I had fallen asleep on the bus and this was all a dream.

Before I got to the form room, Kirsty pulled me into a cleaner's cupboard. Ash was already in there. I asked him if this was his other Fortress of Solitude.

He was like, 'Yeah, I have one indoor and one outdoor.'

I said, 'That seems like cheating.'

'Never mind that.' Kirsty whacked me on the shoulder. 'That video of yours was the funniest thing I have EVER seen.'

'What video?' I said. 'That one where I sit there and talk to the camera? But you already saw that last week.'

She looked at Ash and shook her head. 'What are you talking about, you gomper? I'm talking about that bushcraft one. Oh my God, I actually did a little wee. I showed my brothers and sisters and they all laughed, too. They've all shared it on their Facebook pages and this morning, it made it onto the Web's Funniest Videos.'

No, no, NO! How could this have happened? I never uploaded it. Then I remembered something. I left it on the other tab when Mary was watching *Peter the Pirate*. She must have clicked upload. My life was ruined.

I grabbed Kirsty's phone off her. 'Let me see.'

I clicked the YouTube app and logged onto the Lugs channel. There it was. With ten thousand views.

My stomach flipped. Ten thousand. And five hundred and sixty likes.

I went, 'I-I can't believe it,' all stuttery-like.

Ash said, 'To be fair, it was pretty classic. I mean, you named yourself Cougar, for Krypton out loud.'

I said, 'What's wrong with Cougar? It's a fearsome big cat.'

Kirsty couldn't believe it. 'Why is it that you're the one from a big town, and yet it's us country bumpkins that are teaching you about the world?'

Ash clapped his hand on my shoulder and told me that basically, a cougar is another name for an older woman who fancies young men. I couldn't believe it.

Kirsty spluttered with laughter and said, 'It's true. My Auntie Leslie's boyfriend is ten years younger than her and she calls herself a cougar all the time! She's even got a sticker for her car!'

I said, 'I feel sick.'

Kirsty said, 'Why, have you been munching red berries again?'

Ash applauded and was like, 'Perfectly safe red berries.'

I went pale and my knees started to shake. I scrolled down to the comments.

> **This is the funniest thing I've seen in years.**
> Reply · 👍 👎

> **It's about time someone took the mick out of that pompous idiot, Panther Bliimmington-Weltby.**
> Reply · 👍 👎

> **A perfect parody.**
> Reply · 👍 👎

Kirsty stopped laughing. She said, 'Wait a minute. Were you actually trying to make a serious bushcraft video?'

I wouldn't make eye contact, and was all, 'No, of course not. I knew I was being funny . . . Ha. Ha. Ha.'

Kirsty screamed with laughter. It properly made my ears ring. She went, 'OH MY GOD THAT IS THE FUNNIEST THING I HAVE EVER HEARD. You HAVE to make more. Maybe you're going to be a big time YouTube celebrity after all.'

When I got home that night, I checked my ad revenue. Nothing. Not a penny. I googled it and apparently you need fifty thousand subscribers to make any money from the ads. I had twenty thousand.

I knew I had to make more videos if I had any hope of this plan working.

BACK IN NO TIME

As soon as I got home, I went back on the video editor and pulled together all the stuff I edited out of the original video. Things like me trying to take honey out of a wasp's nest and rubbing two sticks together to make a fire but having to stop because I got splinters.

At about midnight, I sneaked out of the house with the torch. I felt like Aleksandr Kalishnikov in *Soviet Spy Games*. I crept into the outhouse and checked my stats. The second video already had four hundred views and I had thirty thousand subscribers. At this rate, Mum was going to be back in no time.

Me, Kirsty, and Ash were walking to D & T the next afternoon. I prayed to God that we weren't learning whittling.

I heard someone calling me from across the corridor. Except they weren't saying 'Nelson', they were saying 'Cougar'. I ignored it, just like I ignored the constant HILARIOUS jibes of 'thorn face' and 'wee head'.

It was like, 'OI, COUGAR. GET HERE, I WANT TO TALK TO YOU.'

Yep. Marshall Cremaine. I stopped and looked at Kirsty and Ash. I said, 'What do you think he wants?'

Kirsty said, 'I don't know, Cougar. Maybe he's jealous that you have such a tough guy nickname?'

I turned around. Marshall stood there, cracking his knuckles and sneering. He said, 'I've seen your stupid videos. And I don't think they're funny.'

I didn't know what to say. I mean, they weren't supposed to be funny.

'And I'm starting to think that you ain't really a karate master, either.'

I gulped.

Kirsty jumped to my defence, going, 'Yeah, he is. Didn't you see how he broke that tree branch with his head? You have to be trained to do that kind of thing.'

'Hey, shut up!' he yelled at her.

Adrenaline surged through my body and my pulse went BANG BANG BANG. I stepped up and warned him not to talk to Kirsty like that.

His piggy face creased into a smile. He went, 'What, you fancy her or something? Do you want your eyes testing?'

I said, 'Take that back.'

Marshall chuckled to himself and said, 'Make me.'

I pushed him. Yeah, I know. I pushed an enormous gorilla bully. What was wrong with me? Everyone on the corridor stopped, spooked. A murmur went around. Whispers of 'fight' pinged off the walls. Damn. I had triggered an end-of-level boss showdown and didn't have enough ammo. This was worse than when I had to fight the Cthulhu with a Swiss army knife in *Empire of Doom*.

I didn't know what to do. I'd never been in a real fight in my life. Luckily, there was an interruption.

'Uh, huh, what's goin' on here?'

Mr Tronk appeared in the doorway, his shades pushed down his nose.

Marshall grunted. 'Nothing, sir.'

Tronk raised an eyebrow at me. 'Is that right, Nelson?'

I looked at Marshall, then back at Tronk. I said, 'Yes, sir, that's right.'

End-of-level boss neutralized. For now.

BE FUNNY

I tried to stay out of Marshall's way after that. That 'this ain't over' look he gave me after Mr Tronk intervened did not look good.

'You were a total hero,' Kirsty said to me at lunch time. 'DON'T TALK TO HER LIKE THAT. BAAAAAAM!'

I asked if I was an even better hero than Superman. Ash nearly choked on his smiley face potato waffle. Me saying I'm not wussy enough to be allergic to a bit of green rock only made him worse. Kirsty quickly changed the subject before Ash could get going with one of his boring rants, and asked me when they could expect more Cougar videos. I was a bit shocked. I mean, how many are you supposed to do?

She said, 'Loads if you want to get a following. At one time, Darston put a new video up every other day.' She leaned her head on her hand. 'Sometimes, I watch twenty at a time. He is BEAUTIFUL.'

I ignored her prattling about pretty boy Darston and thought about my strategy. I needed to make a video even funnier than the last two. It wasn't going to be easy.

After dinner that night (horrible fish from Scarfwick) I headed outside to start filming my latest video. I just kept thinking: 'Be funny. Be funny.'

ME: Hey, bushcraft lovers, welcome to *Living in the Wild* with me, the biggest baddest cat in the jungle, Cougar Lambsley. I live in the woods and I hunt game, birds, and young MEN! That was a joke!

THE CAMERA CUTS TO THE STREAM.

ME: All right. Now I'm going to make my way across this treacherous river via the slippery stepping stones of doom. One false move and I will be swept away by the undertow and literally drowned to death.

I THEN STAND ON THE FIRST STEPPING STONE, FLAP MY ARMS AROUND AND FALL INTO THE STREAM. IT COMES UP TO MY ANKLE.

ME: That's it—I'm done for!

MARY APPEARS ON CAMERA, HOLDING GERTRUDE UNDER HER ARM.

MARY: Arrrr mateys. Peter the Pirate and his chicken are here to save you! Get him, Gertrude!

MARY PUTS GERTRUDE IN THE STREAM AND I HAVE TO FISH HER OUT BECAUSE SHE HASN'T YET LEARNED THAT CHICKENS CAN'T SWIM.

The video carries on like that for a while. It seemed pretty funny. Maybe. I was beginning to think I didn't know what was funny any more. A lack of TV will do that to you, I guess.

I let Mary watch some cartoons before I uploaded my video. I had more subscribers, but the growth seemed to be slowing down. This video would be the thing that would move me to the next level. Soon, I would be YouTube-famous and Mum will have no choice but to get in touch.

Dad was reading the new Panther Blimmington-Weltby when I went back inside. He offered to show me how to catch and skin a rabbit. He said the easiest way was to sneak up on it and whack it on the back of the head.

We need Mum back, fast.

A MISERABLE OLD WITCH

The next morning I asked the guys what they thought of my latest video.

Kirsty screwed her nose up and said, 'It was OK.'

Just OK? I was a bit gutted, to be honest. I'd actually put loads of effort into this one. I even inserted some comedy sound effects when I fell over and stuff.

Kirsty was like, 'Actually, it was a bit of a let-down after the first two.'

I looked to Ash for support. I didn't get any. He told me I was trying too hard to be funny and that it kind of ruined the magic. I didn't understand.

Kirsty put her hand on my shoulder and said, 'I think you're funnier when you're not trying to be. Sorry.'

That was just their opinion, though. I knew my subscribers might feel differently. I borrowed Kirsty's phone and checked. My heart sank—I was down by nearly five thousand!

Kirsty said, 'YouTube subscribers are a fickle lot. You have to stay on top of your game or you're dead.'

Ash nodded in agreement.

My brain hurt. How was I supposed to get a big enough following to get my mum back when it was so difficult to stay any good? I had a look at the comments to see if I could get some constructive feedback. No such luck.

THIS SUX.
Reply · 👍 👎

U SUCK.
Reply · 👍 👎

NOT FUNNY. SUCKY.
Reply · 👍 👎

I gulped down the brick in my throat. Maybe this whole YouTube thing was a stupid idea. Maybe I would never see my mum again. I felt more miserable than Stanford Jones did after he got stranded on Mars in *Alien Meltdown*.

When Mary and I got home that night, Dad was waiting for us in what was, for him, a pretty smart suit. Well, it didn't have varnish stains on it, anyway.

He was all, 'Welcome back, my children. I am off out tonight to the Annual British Whittling Association Meeting in Norwich.'

Oh, that. I remembered him mentioning it before, but I might have fallen asleep with my eyes open.

I said, 'We haven't got to go with you, have we?'

Dad chuckled and said, 'No, you will stay here with your babysitter.'

Without thinking, I said, 'Ah great, Primrose!'

Dad was like, 'Who is Primrose?'

Oh.

Dad huffed, 'Wait. Do you mean that INTERNET woman? I would never allow such a person in my house.'

Mary looked up from her colouring book and asked if Mummy was coming back to look after us.

Dad went all snappy and said, 'No. It's Mrs Scarfwick.'

I said, 'Mrs Scarfwick? As in the harbourmaster's wife? She's not sweary as well, is she?'

Dad shook his head and said, 'No. But she does have a . . . condition.'

I tried to stop myself from laughing. 'What condition is this?'

'It is called narcolepsy,' Dad said.

I was like, 'Ugghh my God, isn't that where you get nasty scabs and your arms fall off?'

Dad rolled his eyes and said, 'That's leprosy you're thinking of. Narcolepsy is a condition where the sufferer can fall asleep at any time.'

Mary giggled and said, 'Even when she's driving?'

Dad nodded.

'How about if she's on a tightrope over a big bottomless pit?'

Dad was like, 'Uhhhh, yes.'

'How about—'

'Anyway,' Dad interrupted before she could list eighty

zillion other examples. 'If she does fall asleep, just give her a poke. If she won't wake up go and fetch Mr Scarfwick. He can usually rouse her.'

I said, 'What does he do, scream rude words at her?'

Dad nodded.

'So if he is unavailable, could I do that?'

Dad frowned and said 'OK, but only if you absolutely have to.'

Awesome—a licence to swear.

About half an hour later, Mrs Scarfwick arrived. She certainly wasn't as pretty as Primrose. She had all these warts on her face and her mouth was all wrinkly and her hair all grey. Now, I wouldn't have cared about that, but she was horrible on the inside, too.

As soon as Dad left, she was all, 'Get to your bedrooms and I'll call you when dinner's ready.'

She slapped a bag of stinky, blood-soaked fish down on the kitchen table.

'Oh, but Mrs Scarfwick, can't I go outside and play with Gertrude?' Mary asked.

You should have seen her face—you'd have thought Mary had asked if she could kick her in the bum. She barked something about how little girls shouldn't talk back to their elders and Mary started crying straight away. I held her hand and took her up to my room. I managed to cheer her up by doing impressions of Mrs Scarfwick.

'Uggghhh, go away, I'm a miserable old witch. Ughhhhh.'

Mary wiped her eyes and started giggling. She joined in with her own impersonations. I had to keep reminding her to be quiet or the Wicked Witch might hear her. I glanced at my watch. We seemed to have been upstairs for ages. In fact, I couldn't smell dinner cooking, and those fish were so pongy that we would have. I crept downstairs and peeped around the corner. Mrs Scarfwick was sitting in a chair bolt upright, fast asleep.

I went to fetch Mary and told her to keep quiet. When she saw Mrs Scarfwick, she gasped and whispered, 'Oh my gosh, is she deaded?'

I said, 'No, she's just sleeping.'

Mary grinned and said, 'Can we go outside and see Gertrude?'

I nodded. When we got out, I realized how hungry I was. Even though those fish looked horrible, I could still have eaten them. Then I remembered something.

'Mary, do you remember that nice lady from down the lane?'

'The one with the pretty jewellery?'

I said, 'Yeah, how about we go and see her?'

* * *

To begin with, Primrose didn't want to let us in, what with Dad forbidding us and everything, but when Mary told her that horrible Mrs Scarfwick was supposed to be looking after us while Dad was away, she changed her mind. She was cooking herself dinner and added a bit more so we could join her. While she worked, chopping up succulent-looking meat and vegetables, she complimented me on my videos and said that I had talent as a film-maker.

I told her I thought I might have blown it because people didn't seem to like my latest attempt.

Primrose passed me and Mary a glass each. They were filled with this purple juice. It was so sweet, I thought my tongue was going to explode.

Primrose said, 'Don't worry. When you do something creative, it can take a while to figure out what you're good at. I mean, I didn't get good at designing websites overnight. By the way, my clients loved that games site.'

I stopped glugging the delicious brew and gawped. 'Really?'

Primrose told me that it was only fair that I was rewarded, and gave me a crisp twenty pound note from her purse. I wanted to try and refuse it, like polite adults are supposed to do, but I couldn't. It was more money towards the Mum fund, and YouTube wasn't going to make me anything any time soon.

Mary wasn't happy, though, and got all pouty and, 'if Nelson gets a present, I want a present,' about it.

Primrose took off one of her bangles and snipped the end off with some big scissors. Then she blunted the edge with a nail file and pinched it shut around Mary's wrist.

You should have seen Mary's face. It was as if she'd been given a hundred pounds.

The dinner Primrose cooked was delicious. It was chicken in this sweet sauce. It tasted kind of lemony and coconutty and I don't know what, but it was like the most delicious thing ever. Primrose said it was her granny's recipe. She said her grandparents came from Trinidad and they always made great food. She said when she cooked that food, it made her feel like a little kid again. That kind of made me sad because when Mary is older, what will remind her of her childhood? Disgusting fish?

For pudding, Primrose gave us these massive bowls of delicious vanilla, caramel, and chocolate ice cream, with bits of real toffee and chocolate sauce and ohhh, my mouth is watering just thinking about it.

The trouble was, it had been weeks since either of us had really had any sugar, so we were bouncing off the walls. Especially Mary. She re-enacted an entire series of *Peter the Pirate* in thirty seconds.

And it was just as well, because when we saw Dad's headlights coming up the drive, we had to run.

I realized that it would be quicker to pick Mary up, so I gave her a piggyback up to the house. I saw Dad get out of the car, so I sprinted around the side of the house and through the kitchen door. Mary giggled with every bump and I had to shush her. Mrs Scarfwick was still asleep at the table. I saw a long line of dribble hanging out of her mouth and I nearly puked.

I belted into the hall and up the stairs just as Dad came in. I threw Mary onto her bed and then tiptoe-ran into my room and got under the covers.

I didn't sleep much that night—maybe it was because I was on an epic sugar rush, or maybe it was because I got a glimpse of a life I wanted back. And I'm not talking about Mrs Scarfwick.

TO THE EXTREME

I thought we had got away without eating more nasty Scarfwick fish, but Dad rustled them up for breakfast the next morning. He said, 'I think this might become our special tradition. Fish for breakfast on a Saturday.'

Me and Mary exchanged a look. After Primrose's delicious dinner the night before, which was basically like what they must eat in heaven, these fish looked even more revolting.

Dad placed the plates in front of us and was all, 'I was meaning to ask. Didn't either of you have dinner last night?'

I gulped. 'Well, we didn't want to disturb Mrs Scarfwick. She looked all peaceful and that.'

Dad said, 'Hmm, well then you'd better eat all your fish.'

BLLAAARRGGHH!

Mary poked at her plate with her fork and said, 'It tastes like sadness.'

'What was that?' said Dad.

'She said, "it tastes like madness",' I said. 'Like, it's mad how good it is.'

Dad nodded as if that made perfect sense.

I felt like I had to change the subject so I asked him about the whittling thing.

He sat back and smiled, saying, 'It was incredible. All the big names from the world of whittling were there. Exhibitions—the lot. You two would have loved it. Next year we'll all go—have a proper family evening out.'

I tried to arrange my features in a way that said, 'That would be great,' while my brain screamed, 'That would be the worst thing to ever happen to anyone ever.'

Dad wasn't looking at me though. He was looking at Mary. Specifically, her arm. He wanted to know where she got the bangle.

Mary put down her fork, seeming glad for an excuse to stop eating that nasty fish gloop. She said, 'That nice lady—'

'At school,' I interrupted her, quick. 'That nice lady at school, her teacher. She had them making their own bangles. Pretty good isn't it?'

Dad narrowed his eyes at us as if he was trying to see through my lie. After what felt like a week, he said, 'Well, while jewellery doesn't really belong in a rustic way of life, I will allow it as you made it yourself. After all, what kind of whittler would I be if I were to clamp down on crafting?'

I swear if I heard the word 'whittle' one more time, I was going to scream.

Later on I was outside watching Mary play with Gertrude and trying to think of a good idea for another video. What Primrose said about it talking a long time to get good at anything seemed true—I mean, Dad had to practise loads to become a whittling (AAAAAAAARGH) expert. But with YouTubing, it seems like you don't have a chance to fail. People abandon you after one bad video.

What was worse was, I felt like I was forgetting what Mum looked like. It wasn't automatic like before. I had to screw my eyes shut and really try and picture her. I hated that. Dad didn't even have any photos of her up around the house.

I guessed that maybe seeing her made Dad hurt too much, but that didn't mean me and Mary should never see her.

I began to wonder, as I often did, why Mum hadn't been in touch. I mean, yeah, we'd moved to the middle of nowhere, but she could have found us.

Maybe she was just busy. Maybe she was struggling to find the right words.

Maybe she didn't love us any more.

I shook my head really quick to get rid of the thought. How stupid. Of course she still loved us—she was our mum. There had to be a reasonable explanation.

While Dad was sitting outside, whittling (AAAARGH) and watching Mary, I went inside and crept upstairs. We weren't supposed to ever go into Dad's room, but I was breaking so many rules by this point, I thought one more wouldn't hurt. I was Aleksandr Kalishnikov again, infiltrating the Kremlin for my new homeland.

There was an old chest of drawers near the window. The top three drawers had clothes in, but the bottom one was crammed full of papers. I knew there had to be a photo of Mum in there somewhere.

I scooped all the papers and folders out and stacked them. They weren't in any kind of order. Dad always used to be so organized. He even had a filing cabinet at our old house.

None of the stuff in the drawer was useful to me. It was just a load of old bills and whittling (AAAAAAAAARRGGHH) newsletters. I had been through everything. Well, almost everything. There was a small envelope poking out of the corner of the drawer. I pulled it out, being careful not to rip it.

I opened it up and a piece of paper fell out. I picked it up. It was a photo of the four of us, taken on holiday in Spain about a year ago. Mary was wearing water wings and had ice cream all over her face. All of us were smiling. How could it go from that to this in just a year? I kept staring at it, trying to stop the tears in my eyes from making my vision go all blurry.

Heavy footsteps on the stairs. Oh no. I swear my

stomach was trying to jump out of my mouth. I crammed all the papers back into the drawer and tried to close it. The drawer was so full that it was almost overflowing and I had to push really hard before it could close properly.

The bedroom door opened. I lay down, rolled under the bed, and tried to keep still. If Dad found me there would be huge trouble. My pulse throbbed in my neck. Dad seemed to stop and listen. Surely he couldn't hear my heartbeat? He stepped closer to me, then stopped again and turned back.

When I heard his footsteps going back down the stairs, I could breathe again. I put the photo in my pocket and quickly crept back out and downstairs. That was too close.

When I got outside, Dad stared at me with his wild man eyes. He said, 'Where did you get to, son? I was just looking for you.'

I mumbled something about being in my room.

He said, 'Really? You weren't in there a moment ago.'

I swallowed hard. I said, 'That's because I was, um, in my wardrobe. I was taking "getting back to basics" to the extreme.'

Dad gripped my shoulder and grinned. He went, 'I'm glad you're finding new ways to push the boundaries, my boy.'

Once Dad had returned to his work, I went to the outhouse and hid the photo in the hole underneath the laptop.

When I came out, Dad announced that as a special treat tonight, because we'd been doing so well adjusting to our new life, we would drive to the nearest farmers' market and buy some actual food. Oh my God, you have no idea how amazing that sounded. I could have kissed his hairy face. I know it sounds sad, but to us, that was like a trip to Disneyland. Tragic, yeah?

I felt a bit bad because we hadn't been adjusting well at all. We'd been cheating left, right, and centre. Still, the idea of proper food that wasn't foraged or caught by a sweary old fisherman was too good.

We all piled into the car an hour later. Mary started singing the *Peter the Pirate* theme and even Dad joined in as we headed down the drive.

I noticed Primrose at the side of the track, trimming back one of her trees. She turned around, smiled, and waved. Dad grunted something and then slowed the car down.

He was squinting at something on Primrose's arm, glinting in the sunlight. When I realized what it was, my heart nearly stopped.

Dad slammed on the brakes and turned around to look at Mary.

'Mary, did you really get that jewellery from school?'

Mary looked at me, her big green eyes watery and sad. I nodded at her. Then she looked at Dad and burst into tears. Dad grumbled under his breath and jumped out of the car. I followed but I couldn't stop him. He yelled, 'Why did you give jewellery to my daughter?'

Primrose stopped smiling and said, 'You mean why did I give your beautiful little girl a gift?'

Dad's mouth dropped open. 'I don't want you giving my children ANYTHING.'

Dad was crazy mad, but Primrose wasn't intimidated. She folded her arms and said, 'What is your problem, anyway, Mr Lambsley?'

Dad went, 'My problem is that I brought my family out here to escape the wretched filth that you peddle.'

Primrose laughed and said, 'Filth? I'm halfway through designing a website for a teddy bear company.'

Dad snapped a branch off a tree and yelled something about websites being works of evil. Primrose gently took the branch out of Dad's hand and tossed it onto the pile. 'You need to stop with this behaviour,' she said to him. 'Your kids hate the life you're forcing on them.'

Dad growled like an angry dog and yelled, 'They do not! Stop your lying, internet woman!'

Primrose looked at me again and said, 'Tell your father the truth, Nelson.'

I didn't know what to say. I couldn't tell him. He wouldn't be able to handle it. But then how could I stand there in front of Primrose and say everything's fine? I had to find the middle ground. In the end, I just kind of awkwardly said something about the food not being great.

Dad stared at me, his eyes wide with fury. 'Things are finally beginning to make sense. This woman fed you last night, didn't she? When I looked in on Mary last night, she had chocolate around her mouth.'

Damn. Why did she have to be such a messy eater?

Dad said, 'Is this true, Nelson?'

I couldn't keep lying forever about everything. 'Yes,' I said. 'We did.'

'THAT'S IT. NO MORE FARMERS' MARKET TREAT FOR YOU!'

He ordered me back in the car and he reversed it back up the drive at breakneck speed.

I looked out of the window and saw Primrose still watching us, shears in hand. She looked horrified.

When we got home, Dad made Mary take off her bangle, then snapped it in half and threw it away. I tried to stop him but he wouldn't listen. At that moment, I hated him more than I ever hated anyone.

FIGHT!

The next morning, I walked up the path to school, my fists clenching and unclenching. Mary loved that bangle.

When I saw Kirsty and Ash, my mood only got worse. Ash was bent double, coughing. He was covered in green gunk. I asked them what happened.

'Marshall made me go for the Dip,' Ash wheezed.

I was like, 'WHAT? HE PUSHED YOU IN?'

Ash stood up and looked at me. He had that, 'I'm about to puke' look on his face. He said, 'Not exactly. He, um . . . he . . .'

'He made him get in,' said Kirsty. 'He's just lucky I wasn't there!'

I couldn't believe what I was hearing. 'He made you get in? And you just did it?'

'HEY, COUGAR.'

I turned and faced Marshall. This time I wasn't scared at all. I was too angry for that. I stormed up to him and tried my best to get in his face.

Marshall laughed and said, 'You were supposed to take the Dip, Cougar. If you'd have just took it like a man, your wimpy mate wouldn't have had to suffer.'

My insides were a ball of pure fury. My hands shook.

He said, 'I'll tell you something else. That latest video of yours was crap.'

He wasn't the only person with that opinion. In fact, a charming guy called FatNeck4lyfe told me that via YouTube comment that very morning.

He stepped closer, looming over me and telling me I was worthless and pathetic.

I stayed silent, trying to stop the neutron bomb in my brain from ticking down to zero.

Marshall leaned in so close, I could smell his horrible breath. He whispered, 'It's no wonder your mum left you.'

BOOM! It went off. I pushed him. Hard. He smiled. That was exactly the reaction he was after.

END-OF-LEVEL BOSS FIGHT ACTIVATED.

Marshall grabbed me by my collar and slammed me into the wall of the sports hall. The back of my head whacked against the brick. It killed.

A massive crowd gathered around us, urging us on, screaming 'FIGHT!'

I wrenched my arm free. **VULNERABLE AREA DETECTED. DEPLOY WEAPONRY.** I socked Marshall in his fleshy stomach. He doubled over, struggling for breath. The roar of the crowd got louder.

I was unsure of my next move. When I watched fights

on TV (ah, TV, I remember you) they would punch each other in the face, and blood would fly everywhere, and one of them would end up on the floor. As it was, I kind of stood there, saying, 'Yeah, take THAT,' and not knowing what to do next. I got the urge to start mashing controller buttons.

Marshall grabbed my shirt and dragged me to the floor. Three buttons came off in his hand and my pasty chest was on display for the whole world.

We rolled around on the floor as a circle gathered around us. By now, there was a full-blown chant—'FIGHT, FIGHT, FIGHT . . .'

Somehow, I managed to overpower Marshall and ended up on top of him. I was planning on getting up and running away, but then a big pair of hands dragged me off.

'Break it up, break it up, uh huh.'

Mr Tronk pulled us both to our feet. 'Now, tell me what all this fussin' and a-feudin' is about.'

Neither of us said anything. Tronk smoothed his quiff back.

'Then I ain't got no choice but to call your parents.'

'WHAT?'

I sat in reception while Marshall's parents went into Tronk's office. I knew he couldn't get hold of Dad because we didn't have a phone. He'd just have to send a letter, and that could be easily intercepted.

I sat back and closed my eyes. All this video making and fighting can really take it out of a person. My eyes snapped open again when I heard a familiar voice.

'NELSON! WHAT THE DEVIL HAVE YOU BEEN UP TO?'

Standing there in reception, looking like the kind of person you would cross the road to avoid, with his long beard, straggly hair, and varnish-stained 'WHITTLIN' 'TIL I DIE' T-shirt, was Dad.

I was like, 'H-how, did they get hold of you?'

He said, 'Do you think I'd be so negligent to not have an emergency contact for either of you? I gave them the harbour's telephone number.'

I said, 'You mean they called Scarfwick?'

Mrs Grafflaw, the school receptionist, looked at us over her glasses and said, 'Yes we did. And what a frightfully rude man he is, too.'

Mr Tronk's door opened and Marshall emerged, somehow looking smaller than he did before. As he went past, he gave me a sneaky 'I'm going to get you' glance.

Tronk raised an eyebrow and blasted us with a finger pistol.

We sat down opposite Tronk's desk. I'd been in a few teachers' offices before but nothing like this. Books and papers were scattered around as if they'd been dropped from a great height. There were framed photos of Elvis everywhere along with a guitar and gold discs and American flags and a massive jukebox in the corner. There was even a goldfish in a bowl with a neon sign that said **KING** on a shelf above it.

Mr Tronk sat opposite us and steepled his fingers.

'Reason I called you here, Mr Lambsley, is that your boy got into a fight this afternoon. Uh huh.'

Dad shot me a sideways look as if to say, 'Who's this weirdo?' Mr Tronk was probably thinking the same thing.

'Now, Nelson is a good kid,' Tronk went on. 'He works hard, he's polite and heck, I know he didn't start it. Some other kids tell me that the other boy provoked him.'

Dad just sat there, staring.

Tronk went on, 'But I need you to realize that violence ain't the answer, son. If you can promise me this will never happen again, there will be peace in the valley. What say you, Daddy?'

Dad stroked his beard and said, 'In the wild, you must fight off predators.'

I hid my face in my palm.

Tronk said, 'I hear ya. But this ain't the wild, no suh. This is a place of learning and we solve our problems with our minds, not our fists.'

Dad wasn't really going along with it, but eventually he promised to punish me at home.

Mr Tronk looked at me and said, 'Listen to me, Nelson. Whenever you feel like getting angry, go do something else. We've all got that little something that makes us happy. For your daddy, it's whittling, am I right?'

Dad brightened up at the mention of whittling and

nodded enthusiastically.

'And for me, it's singing.'

He jumped up out of his chair and pulled the guitar off a stand attached to the wall. He rested his snakeskin-boot-clad foot on the desk and strummed out a few chords, before singing this super old song called 'Love Me Tender'.

It was so embarrassing. The song was proper cheesy. People would listen to anything in the olden days. I mean, this Elvis was the biggest pop star in the world and he carked it straining on the toilet. What an idiot.

I glanced over at Dad to see if he was as weirded out as I was. His eyes were all wet. I couldn't believe it. Mr Tronk's singing was making him emotional.

When we left the office, Dad stormed back out to the car. He had parked next to Mr Tronk's Cadillac.

Someone shouted at me from the other side of the car park, 'Hey, it's Cougar! When's your next video coming out?'

My heart froze. Dad turned and stared at them. 'What does that mean?'

I snapped, 'NOTHING. Let's go, eh?'

If Dad found out about the videos, I think his head would actually pop.

He sat in the driver's seat but didn't start the car. We still had fifteen minutes before Mary finished school. Dad turned to me and asked if I won the fight. I mean, what kind of question was that? 'It was a draw,' I said.

He shook his head and said, 'Then it is down to me to teach you the ways of combat.'

I know, I know. I decided to change the subject by asking him about that song.

He adjusted the rear-view mirror and fiddled with some change from the cup holder. He said, 'What song?'

I said, 'That one Mr Tronk was singing in the office. You looked . . . sad.'

He said, 'No I didn't,' and wound the window down. I zipped up my coat and shivered.

I went, 'You kind of did, though.'

Dad picked up an old parking sticker off the dashboard and rubbed it between his fingers. His hands were cracked and dirty, with streaks of varnish and God knows what else all over them. His fingernails were thick and black. I remembered when he used to keep his hands in top condition all the time. Once, he even got a manicure. I teased him about it, but he told me that people don't buy houses from agents with scruffy hands.

He turned and looked at me, still holding the sticker. He said, 'It was mine and your mum's first dance at our wedding.'

He wound the window back up and rubbed his eyes. It was dead quiet.

'Where is she, Dad?' I asked him.

Dad sighed and began to tear the sticker into tiny pieces. He said, 'I don't know. All I know is that she has left us all in the lurch. At least now, we are living better and more authentically. We are happier.'

I said, 'Are we, though?'

He said, 'YES. Anyway, it's time to pick up your sister. And I don't want her to hear about any of this.'

We didn't speak for the rest of the journey.

THE WAYS OF COMBAT

I didn't see Marshall at school the next day. Maybe he had been suspended. Or he was scared I would totally pound him. Yeah, he was probably suspended.

Kirsty was loving it at lunchtime. She said, 'You are totally my hero, Nelson. Fighting Marshall Cremaine. Wow.'

Ash stared at his plate and jabbed at a pile of mashed potatoes with his fork. He probably felt like a wuss for getting in the brook. He wouldn't tell Tronk about it either because Marshall promised to get him if he did.

I said, 'I only did it because he said something about my mum.'

Kirsty gasped and said, 'Well then you practically had to fight him. It's the law.'

Mum wouldn't have wanted me fighting over her, though. Then again, who knows what she would have wanted? She disappeared.

Kirsty gently shook my shoulder. I must have been staring into space again. 'Are you OK, Nels? Is the lack of telly making you go mad? Or worse, is it making your dad go mad?'

I asked what she meant. I was beginning to worry that this was a real possibility.

Kirsty leaned forward and whispered. 'Have you ever seen a film called *The Shining*?'

I'd never heard of it.

She wiped her mouth with the back of her hand and leaned in closer still. She said, '*The Shining* is the greatest film of all time. My dad's got it on Blu-Ray and I sometimes watch it when everyone's in bed.'

I asked Ash if he'd seen it.

Kirsty was like, 'Don't even bother asking him. If it hasn't got a bloke in a cape and underpants in it, he's not interested.'

Ash went to argue, then shrugged and went back to his mash.

She said, '*The Shining* is about a man who looks after this hotel in the mountains with his wife and son. Eventually, he starts to go mad and sees ghosts everywhere.'

I gulped. 'Then what?'

Kirsty dropped her voice even lower, that crazy look still in her eyes. 'Eventually, he completely flips and starts chasing his family around the hotel with an axe.'

I know. What a friend.

'You don't have an axe in your house, do you, Nels?' she asked.

I made a mental note to hide it as soon as I got home. Forget firewood, I'd rather be cold than chopped up.

That evening, I got my camera and went straight into the woods to make another video. I needed Mum back straight away before Dad went all Shining on us. Watching clips from the film on YouTube did nothing to make me feel better, either. Anyway, I tried to put it out of my mind as I sat on a tree stump and looked down the lens.

ME: Hello everyone, Cougar Lambsley here. Now, I know a lot of you didn't like my latest video. Sorry about that. Seems like I can only be funny when I'm not trying to be. How weird is that? Anyway, it's time for me to be completely honest with you. There is a reason I am making these videos. I want my mum back. To begin with, I thought making loads of money off YouTube would get her to come back, but I've been trying to make videos for ages and at this rate it's going to take me about three thousand years to get enough cash.

So I'm going to have to be more straightforward, Can you find her for me? She looks like this.

I REACH BEHIND ME AND PULL OUT THE PHOTO I TOOK FROM DAD'S DRAWER.

ME: Her name is Jenny Lambsley. She is about five foot six, she likes yoga, um, I thought she did, anyway. She has green eyes, and—

I HEAR FOOTSTEPS COMING THROUGH THE WOODS AND I QUICKLY DROP THE PHOTO BEHIND THE STUMP.

DAD: Ah, there you are, son.

I FREEZE AND LOOK AT THE CAMERA SITTING ON A BRANCH IN A TREE. MY EXPRESSION SEEMS TO SAY 'IF DAD SEES THAT, IM DONE FOR.'

DAD: Have you seen my axe?

HE STROKES HIS LONG, STRAGGLY BEARD.

ME: Um, no. I haven't.

DAD: We need wood for the fire. The air is cold. Without it, we will surely perish.

DAD WALKS OVER AND SITS NEXT TO ME.

DAD: I've been meaning to talk to you, my boy.

ME: (Panicking) Oh yes? What about? Something indoorsy? Let's go indoors and talk about it.

DAD: No. This can only be discussed out here. In the wild. In the majesty of nature.

141

I SNEAK A LOOK AT THE CAMERA.

DAD: It is time for you to learn the ways of combat.

ME: (Pinching the bridge of my nose) How about another time? I have a headache.

DAD: (Jumping to his feet) Nonsense! That school of yours is teeming with predators. Your only hope of getting through it is by learning how to take them on. Now get up.

ME: What?

DAD RAISES HIS EYEBROWS AT ME AND I STAND.

DAD: (Pacing backwards and forwards) Question. What is the most fearsome animal in the forest?

ME: I haven't seen that many here, so I'm going to say the squirrel.

DAD: No, not this forest, I mean the forest of LIFE!

ME: (Pondering) Man?

DAD: Don't be ridiculous. How can Man be the deadliest animal?

ME: Um, because they can make guns and bombs and stuff like that.

DAD: You are not thinking about this the right way, my boy. The deadliest animal is the bear. I mean, yes, the human may have a gun, but he doesn't have a big massive paw that can smash your face off.

ME: What are you talking about?

DAD: If you are to avoid any further losses in combat, you must learn to be like the bear.

I LOOK DOWN AT MY SCRAWNY BODY, REALIZING I AM THE LEAST BEAR-LIKE PERSON IN THE WORLD.

ME: Well, actually, I didn't lose the fight, it was a draw.

DAD HUFFS OUT THROUGH HIS NOSE, THEN GOES UP ON HIS TIPTOES AND ROARS LIKE A BEAR. I TRY TO RUN BUT HE WRAPS HIS ARMS AROUND ME AND PICKS ME UP.

DAD: THIS IS THE BEAR HUG. It will incapacitate your enemy and leave them dazed!

ME: Aaargh!

DAD: Raaaaaaaaaarrrr!

ME: I can't breathe!

DAD: Feel the power of the bear!

I START TURNING BLUE AND BLACKING OUT SO DAD PUTS ME DOWN.

DAD: Now you try.

ME: (Gasping for breath) Yeah, right!

DAD: DO IT!

ME: Fine!

I GRAB HIM. MY HANDS BARELY MEET ON THE OTHER SIDE.

DAD: PUNY!

DAD PICKS ME UP ABOVE HIS HEAD AND SPINS ME AROUND. PART OF ME IS KIND OF THRILLED, BECAUSE IT REMINDS ME OF BEING A LITTLE KID, BUT ANOTHER PART OF ME THINKS HE'S GONE FULL-BLOWN SHINING AND IS ABOUT TO SMASH ME UP A TREE. I WRIGGLE FREE AND SCRAMBLE AWAY FROM HIM.

ME: Will you just leave me alone? I don't want to be a bear!

DAD BREATHES DEEPLY AND NODS.

DAD: OK, son. But this is not the last time I will try to teach you the ways of combat.

ME: Whatever.

DAD WALKS AWAY INTO THE WOODS AND I STAND THERE, TRYING TO GET MY BREATH BACK. I AM ABOUT TO TURN THE CAMERA OFF, WHEN A SUDDEN CRY OF 'UNEXPECTED BEAR ATTACK!' NEARLY MAKES ME HAVE A CARDIAC ARREST AND DAD BURSTS OUT OF THE WOODS, SCOOPS ME UP IN HIS ARMS, AND SCREAMS 'THE ELEMENT OF SURPRISE!'

I watched the video back on the laptop. It was so ridiculous, there was no way I could publish it. Imagine what people like Marshall would say at school after they

watched me being chucked around a forest by my mad, beardy dad. No, back to the drawing board. I would try again tomorrow.

I was about to press delete, but I stopped. Maybe I was being too hasty. Maybe this video could act as a cry for help? A kind of, 'I need to find my mum because look at what I have to put up with' thing? I didn't want to get Dad in trouble, but enough was enough.

I went backwards and forwards all through the editing process. Even as I stared at the loading screen, I still didn't know if it was a good idea.

Come on, do you want your mum back or not? I thought. You owe it to Mary to do something.

I took a deep breath and pressed upload.

GRIZZLY DADAMS

Before we set off for school the next morning, I checked my stats for that video. I'd already had three hundred views and some comments.

> **Ur dad is a mentalist.**
> Reply · 👍 👎

> **U shud have dropped the whiny wuss on his hed innit.**
> Reply · 👍 👎

> **This is the funniest one yet! MOAR!**
> Reply · 👍 👎

Great, I thought. So people aren't seeing this as a cry for help at all. They think it's funny. Would they find it so hilarious if they had to live with him?

On the way to school, Mary was sulking again. I asked her if she was still upset about the bangle. She shook her head and looked out of the window. Her eyes were all wet and I could tell she was trying not to cry.

I poked her arm and said, 'Well then what is it?'

Her chin started trembling. She went, 'Daddy said we were going to eat Gertrude.'

I was like, 'What?'

She looked at me, and I could tell she was on the verge of a meltdown. She said, 'Daddy told me she was getting fat because I keep feeding her and that she would be nice and juicy.' She stopped and rubbed her eyes. 'I don't want to eat Gertrude.'

I put my arm around her shoulder and promised her I wouldn't let that happen.

I didn't quite know how I would stop him. I thought maybe I could forage us another chicken and hope he wouldn't be able to tell the difference. Or maybe I would volunteer to kill it to prove how rugged I'd become—but I'd just take it out to the woods and then come back with chicken nuggets and say I'd done it. You know, kind of like Snow White.

When I got to school, Kirsty told me she had watched my video and said that my dad was just like the bloke from *The Shining*. Then she asked me if we had a hedge maze. She is weird.

Because of this weirdness, I wasn't that bothered when she ran at me screaming at lunchtime. I just thought she was having one of her moments. Ash followed behind with his fingers in his ears.

I tried to ask what was up, but I couldn't get any sense out of her. She was hyperventilating and her glasses had steamed up. She was making these wacky noises, like, 'Wha, ha, haha, Dar, Dar Dar.'

She grabbed my face in both hands. Her palms were really clammy. I eyeballed Ash and asked if she was having some kind of fit.

Ash shook his head and said, 'You know that Darston bloke she loves?'

I gasped. 'Oh my God, is he dead?'

Ash shook his head and said, 'Show him, Kirst.'

Kirsty pulled out her phone, still blathering and gibbering like a monkey after a can of Red Bull. She clicked on the YouTube app and shoved it in my face.

I recognized the lad talking on screen—Midlake Darston. I said, 'Wow, he really is dreamy.'

Kirsty was like, 'Watch. Just watch,' all raspy and strangulated.

I turned up the volume.

MIDLAKE: Hey guys, MD here. Now, you know I like to think I'm the freshest vlogger around, but sometimes, I have to give credit where credit is due. I watched a video this morning that BLEW MY MIND. This guy has to be the zaniest dude I have ever seen, and I live in LA, so I've seen my share of crazies. His name isn't mentioned on there, so I'm going to call him Grizzly Dadams. I'm not going to say anything else, you need to see it for yourselves.'

Midlake faded out and what replaced him nearly made me faint.

It was me.

Being picked up by my dad.

Then my dad acting like a bear.

'Oh my God,' I said.

Ash could take it no more and burst out laughing until tears rolled down his cheeks. Kirsty grabbed a paper bag off the side and started breathing into it.

I stopped the video and logged onto my channel. I had five thousand more views, over fifty thousand subscribers, nine hundred likes and tons of comments.

Midlake sent me here! LOL.
Reply · 👍 👎

I have watched this twenty times and it NEVER gets old.
Reply · 👍 👎

SURPRISE ATTACK!! HAHAHHAHHAAAAAAAAAAA!
Reply · 👍 👎

I checked my ad revenue. I already had a tenner.

It was then I realized what I needed to do to make enough money to get Mum back.

I wasn't going to be a YouTube celebrity.

My dad was.

BYE BYE, GERTRUDE

I was buzzing that night. Dad must have noticed because he said, 'You look happy tonight, son. Did our combat lesson serve you well?'

'Something like that,' I said.

He smiled and started tucking into his stew. Yep, stew again. Mary didn't eat much of hers. I reckon she could see Gertrude looking up at her from the bowl.

I made a mental list of things to sort out and I had two whole weeks of half term to do them.

1. Solve the chicken problem.
2. Make more secret Grizzly Dadams videos.

I decided to tackle the chicken issue first. When Dad sat down at his whittling table, I took Mary outside, telling Dad we were going foraging.

Once we were out of earshot, I explained my plan to Mary. She wasn't happy that she wouldn't be able to see Gertrude every day, but at least she would be safe.

Mary held Gertrude under her arm and stroked the back of her head. We headed down the track, then turned into the woody bit. We had to approach from behind because we couldn't risk Dad seeing us.

When Primrose answered the door, she didn't seem as happy as before. She was like, 'It's great to see you but you really shouldn't be here. We don't want to get into trouble with your dad, do we?'

I said, 'I know, but we kind of have another favour to ask you.'

Primrose chuckled to herself and said, 'I'm not teaching you how to fight like a bear.'

I was like, 'You've seen the video?'

She said, 'EVERYONE has seen it. About twenty different people have shared it on my Facebook. I mean, I don't find it as funny because I've seen him in the flesh.'

Mary tugged on my trouser leg. 'What are you talking about?'

I said, 'Nothing. Anyway, Primrose, the favour I have to ask you is related to Gertrude.'

She looked confused.

I said, 'Our chicken. I know you have a coop and I was wondering if you could look after her for a while?'

Primrose was like, 'And I'm guessing your dad doesn't know about this?'

I shook my head.

She said, 'Then I'm going to have to say no. If he finds out, he'll accuse me of stealing it.'

I said, 'That won't happen. I promise.'

Primrose said no again. She just didn't need more trouble from Dad. I could understand what she meant. If Dad found Gertrude at Primrose's he would go full-on mental.

Mary's bottom lip began to wobble. Oh God. She was going to start crying. And this wasn't going to be a quiet cry. This was going to be one of those special, 'oh dear Lord is she being murdered?' cries.

'WAAAAAAAHHH, PLEASE TAKE HER MISS PWIMWOSE, DADDY SAYS HE'S GOING TO EAT HER AND I DON'T WANT HER TO DIE SHE'S MY BEST FWIEND AND DADDY TOOK MY BWACELET OFF ME AND I'M WEALLY WEALLY SAD, AAAAAAAARRRGGHH.'

Primrose sighed and kneeled down to Mary's level. She said, 'Please don't cry.' But it was no good. There was no stopping her.

'AAAAAAAAAARGGGHHHHH.'

Primrose gave Mary a hug and said, 'OK fine, I'll look after Gertrude.'

Mary stopped crying and sniffed. 'Really?'

Primrose pulled a hanky out of her pocket, dried Mary's cheeks and said, 'Just no more tears, OK?'

Mary nodded and turned Gertrude around so she

153

was staring her right in the eye. She said, 'Now Gertrude, I want you to be good for Primrose and to play nicely with the other chickens, OK?' She waited for a second and then said, 'Good,' as if Gertrude had answered her.

We went around to the allotment and put Gertrude into Primrose's coop. Mary gave her a kiss goodbye and made me do the same.

She started getting all weepy again so I thought it would be best to get her home. Primrose gave us both a hug and passed us some carrots and apples so it looked like we really had been 'foraging'.

Mary made me promise that we would go and visit all the time. It seemed like half-term would involve more sneaking around than I thought.

CHICKEN THIEF

The first thing I heard the next morning was shouting from outside. I shot out of bed, scared that I might be missing valuable Grizzly Dadams footage.

I ran outside in my pyjamas and asked Dad what was up. He looked mad, all wild-eyed and sweaty. He was ranting something about there being a 'chicken thief in our midst.'

I tried to seem shocked and slipped away to the outhouse. I grabbed the camera from out of the hole and wrapped it in an old sack. I made sure that the lens was sticking out, but not too much. Luckily, the sack was dark grey and it blended in. I switched the camera on and went back out.

Dad eyeballed me weird and asked why I was carrying a sack.

I said, 'Because if I find the chicken, I will use it to scoop it up.'

Mary came outside in her pyjamas, rubbing her eyes and wanting to know what was happening.

I gave her a sly wink and told her Gertrude had gone

missing and we were looking for her.

She said, 'Ohhhhh,' and gave me a wink that was about as subtle as a cricket bat to the face.

Dad stopped and sniffed the air. He said, 'I know who has taken our chicken.'

My stomach went all fluttery. Surely he couldn't have smelled me out?

Dad licked his finger and held it up. He said, 'The chicken's natural predator. The fox.'

Phew.

Dad paced around, saying, 'We must hunt the fox down and punish him so he cannot take more of our livestock.'

I said, 'Right. Well, you know, lead on.'

Dad nodded and headed into the woods. I followed, clutching the camera tight. The whole time, my head whirled with a mixture of emotions. Part of me was scared that my dad was becoming more and more insane, and getting further and further away from the person he used to be. But another part was massively excited because I knew this was going to be the best video ever.

A DECENT SUPPLY OF HENS

After a week of secret filming, I had a video ready to upload. By this time, Dad had given up looking for foxes and said he was thinking about buying a cow. I gulped. There was no way I'd be able to hide one of those.

I sat down to upload the video on Sunday night, my inbox bulging with demands for more videos. Grizzly Dadams was becoming more and more popular. There were even Facebook fan pages appearing.

I clicked onto one of them. It had two thousand likes. I sent the admin a message saying a new video had been uploaded. My ad revenue had reached fifty quid. Not exactly a fortune, but it was heading in the right direction. I knew another quality video could push me up even further. I was wary after last time of ruining it by trying to be too funny. But this was different—Dad had no idea he was being filmed so he wasn't playing up to the cameras. He was just being his normal, crazy self. In the end, this was the video.

DAD STANDS IN THE MIDDLE OF THE WOODS.

DAD: To catch the fox, we must act like the fox.

DAD GETS DOWN ON HIS KNEES AND MAKES THIS WEIRD NOISE, WHICH HE THINKS SOUNDS LIKE A FOX BUT ACTUALLY SOUNDS MORE LIKE A GOOSE BEING STRANGLED.

DAD: Show yourself, fox. Come and face FOREST JUSTICE! Wrrrraaaaaaaaaaggghhhh.

DAD SITS IN THE LOUNGE, WHITTLING.

DAD: To whittle is to become God-like. For what are we if not whittled from the stuff of creation? If there is a God, he is the greatest whittler of all.

DAD STANDS BY THE SIDE OF THE STREAM.

DAD: When we hunt, it is important that we blend in with our surroundings.

DAD SCRAPES HIS HANDS ALONG THE BED OF THE STREAM AND COVERS HIS FACE IN MUD.

DAD: I am now completely camouflaged. No one will be able to see me.

SCARFWICK WALKS INTO SHOT WITH AHAB THE DOG.

SCARFWICK: BLEEPing BLEEP, man, what's all that BLEEP you've got on your face, you DAFT BLEEPing BLEEPer?

DAD STANDS IN THE KITCHEN COOKING YET ANOTHER STEW.

DAD: Interesting you should ask, my boy. This stew is made entirely from things that grow in my garden. It has my carrots, leeks, potatoes, and nettles.

DAD SAMPLES A SPOONFUL FROM THE PAN

ME: Nettles? Like stinging nettles.

DAD'S FACE TWISTS UP.

DAD: Can you fetch me a glass of water, son? And

why are you carrying that sack around everywhere?

DAD CREEPS UP ON A HOLE IN THE GROUND.

DAD: (Whispering) Look, son. I have finally located the home of the fox. Now the hunter becomes the hunted.

DAD DRAWS HIS HOME-MADE SLINGSHOT AND AIMS IT AT THE HOLE. HE FIRES A PELLET, WHICH BOUNCES OFF A ROCK AND HITS HIM IN THE FACE. WHILE HE HOLDS HIS NOSE AND SWEARS, THE FOX EMERGES FROM THE HOLE AND RUNS AWAY.

I uploaded it the same night. Within two days, it had three hundred thousand views. I uploaded more and the views kept going up and up. I couldn't believe it—my dad was a true YouTube star and he had no idea.

People were even making parodies of it. There was one where Darth Vader was prancing around a forest acting like a fox. A couple of guys from Australia made a reaction video—which was just them sitting watching it and laughing. This website called ViralMania rated it third in their 'Most Mental Vids Chart'.

I was just reading an article speculating about Grizzly

Dadams's true identity when the door opened. It was only Mary, but I nearly had a heart attack.

She wasn't happy. With no chicken around to play with, she was bored, and me spending all my time on videos wasn't exactly helping.

I placed all the forbidden equipment back in the hole and we ducked out. I was going to tell Dad that we were going for a walk, but he was up a tree trying to catch a pigeon. He was doing pigeon calls and everything. I wished I was filming him.

Anyway, me and Mary headed down the road to see our chicken. Primrose came out with glasses of pop. The sweet goodness of it exploded in my mouth. At home, it was water or some kind of tea that wasn't made with a teabag, and you ended up with all these minging leaves stuck in your teeth.

Mary named all the other chickens, Elsa, Nancy, and Jenny. She said, 'Jenny is my mummy's name. Nelson is going to get her to come home, aren't you, Nelson?'

I said, 'Course I am.'

Mary grinned and started running around the garden with her feathered army.

'About that,' said Primrose. 'Have you ever thought of putting a photo of her in one of your videos? Then, if

161

someone knows where she is, they can get in touch.'

I swallowed a mouthful of delicious lemonade and said, 'I was about to do that, but then Dad turned up and started acting all bear-like. I'll definitely do it on my next one.'

Primrose said, 'Make sure they send proof, though. You don't want to be fooled by trolls.'

I knew all about trolls. One commented that he was going to find Dad and show him real combat. Good luck to him.

I was about to drop a hint for another glass of the sweet stuff, when I heard a voice on the other side of the trees.

It was calling my name.

Oh no. I ran after Mary and picked her up in one arm and a chicken I sincerely hoped was Gertrude in my other and hid in Primrose's shed.

Mary was all, 'I don't like it in here, it's dark and smelly.'

I put my finger to my lips and whispered. 'This is part of our top secret mission. We have to hide from Daddy. Otherwise he'll find out what happened to Gertrude.'

Gertrude looked at Mary and clucked. I shushed her, but she didn't seem to understand what that meant.

I sneaked a look out of the shed window. Dad was standing on Primrose's back-door step, his hands on his hips, saying, 'I see you still have a decent supply of hens.'

Primrose agreed and said something about how you can't beat fresh eggs. I think she meant like they were good, 'cause you totally can beat eggs.

Dad was like, 'I wouldn't know as my hen has gone missing. In fact . . .' He scanned Primrose's birds and seemed to zone in on one that had similar colouring to Gertrude. 'Ah ha!'

He picked up the chicken and held it close to his face. 'Surely my own neighbour cannot be stealing from me!'

Primrose rubbed her face as if she was tired and said, 'I can assure you, Mr Lambsley, I did not steal your chicken.'

Dad held up a hand to silence her, never taking his eye from the chicken's face. I can't be sure, but I think it was Elsa.

He was like, 'Hmm, you're right. I knew that chicken well, and this isn't the same one.'

Primrose smiled and said, 'You knew the chicken well?'

Dad put the hen back down and turned to face Primrose. He said, 'Of course. When you are truly at one with nature, you can commune with all its creatures.'

I could tell Primrose was trying not to laugh. I thought about all the thousands of people who would have given their left kidneys to have been able to witness this first-hand.

Primrose said, 'Is that right?'

Dad said, 'Of course it is! Still, I don't expect an internet charlatan like you to understand such things.'

Primrose walked towards Dad. 'What do you have against the internet, anyway?'

Dad looked furious, like he was about to blow. Mary poked me in the leg and asked me what was happening. I shushed her and tried to listen.

Dad huffed. 'I hate the internet because it is ruining the world! It corrupts everything! It makes a mockery of tradition . . . and love . . . and . . . family.'

Primrose stepped even closer to him. I squinted through the dirty plastic window. It looked like he was crying. Oh my God.

Primrose hugged Dad. He tried to push her away for a second, but then gave up and hugged her back. I could see his shoulders jerking up and down. Why would talking about the internet make him cry? There was so much I didn't understand.

I could see Primrose talking to him but I couldn't quite hear her. It seemed like she was saying, 'It's OK,' a lot.

Suddenly, Dad broke the hug and yelled, 'NO! Let go of me, internet woman!' And then he stomped back up the track to our house.

When I was sure the coast was clear, me, Mary, and Gertrude came out of our hiding place. I put Gertrude back in the pen with the others.

'I think you need to go home and see your dad,' Primrose said to us.

'What's the matter with him?' I asked.

She sighed. 'He's a very . . . hurt man.'

'HURT?' said Mary. 'Did you beat him up?'

When we got home, Dad was busy making a cabinet out of wood. He did it super quick as if he were a robot. He asked us where we had been, never looking up from his work. I told him we had just been for a walk in the woods. I found lying easier because he was avoiding eye contact.

'I went into your outhouse,' Dad said.

I stopped. My guts twisted. No. Oh God no. What was I going to do?

He nodded as he hammered and said, 'Yes. It looks like an excellent place to study. Well done.'

I relaxed slightly. He hadn't found the secret stash. I looked closely at Dad's face. His eyes were all puffy. He really had been crying.

I thought if I could get Mum back, it would cheer him up. And maybe encourage him to shave that beard off. I mean, it was horrible. This once he had a whole carrot in there and didn't even realize. I decided to take Primrose's advice and put that photo of Mum out there. Once Mary was in bed, I went out and scraped the last of the footage together, then put that photo of Mum at the end, with a message that said—

HAVE YOU SEEN THIS WOMAN? LEAVE A MESSAGE WITH ANY INFO.
Reply · 👍 👎

When I closed the laptop I said a little prayer. I'm not that religious, but I thought it might help. Maybe someone out there would know where Mum was. Dad was wrong—internet people were good, helpful souls who were always quick to assist someone in need.

Yeah, right.

GRIZZLY DADAMS JR

School was a different place when I went back. Well, it wasn't actually a different place—it was still the same school. It just felt different.

People kept staring at me. A couple of Year Nines even asked me for my autograph. I mean, they made me write 'Grizzly Dadams Jr' but it still counts.

The first thing I felt when I walked into my form room was all the air being squeezed out of my lungs. With the last of my breath, I asked Kirsty what the hell she was doing to me.

'Giving you a bear hug!' she growled. 'Raaaaa-aaaaaaarrrr!'

I prised her arms from around me. She is surprisingly strong.

I was like, 'Yeah, cheers, I actually just want to sit down, thanks.'

Kirsty jabbed me in the ribs and said, 'Did you know you were on telly this morning?'

'Course he doesn't,' said Ash. 'He doesn't have one.'

Kirsty stuck her tongue out at Ash and accessed the

LOL of the Week website on her phone. You know, that TV show that compiles all the funniest YouTube clips of the week? Grizzly Dadams was on it and I had no idea.

'This is mad,' I said.

Kirsty was like, 'NOT AS MAD AS YOUR DAD! We HAVE to meet him.'

Ash nodded so hard, I thought his head was going to fly off.

I flat out refused.

'Aw, come on,' said Kirsty, pulling her 'pwetty pwease' face.

'NO.' I took a book about the Industrial Revolution out of my bag and pretended to be super interested in it.

'Fine,' I heard Kirsty say. 'We might not be allowed to come to his house, but there's no crime in getting on his bus is there?'

I groaned into my book.

Ash said, 'No, there isn't. And if we happen to stumble upon a house while we're out hiking in the woods and ask the man of the house for directions, then what's the harm in that?'

I slammed the book down and looked right at them. I said, 'You are not doing this. Forget it.'

I'VE NEVER MET A CELEBRITY BEFORE

On the bus home, Mary tapped my shoulder and said, 'Who are those two people sitting behind us?'

I turned around and growled at Kirsty and Ash, who sat there looking like they were about to have all their Christmases rolled into one. I was like, 'I don't know. They must have got on the wrong bus.'

I couldn't believe they were actually going to do this. Maybe if I grabbed Mary and ran off into the woods, I could lose them, I thought. Then I realized that doing that would make me look like some kind of creepy murderer.

When we got off the bus, Ash and Kirsty followed us. I turned around and asked them if their parents would be wondering where they were, hoping that would get rid of them. No such luck. Kirsty was all, 'Nah, we've told them that we're going to our friend's house and we'll be getting the bus home.'

I cursed under my breath and carried on.

'Look, you can't come,' I said over my shoulder. 'Go down to the harbour instead—you'll learn some new swear words.'

They carried on following me.

When we reached the dirt track, we found Dad cutting branches off trees. My heart sank.

He was like, 'Good afternoon, children. I am just gathering firewood for tonight's dinner. We will be roasting fish over an open flame.'

I tried to gulp down the puke eruption in my mouth. Dad looked at Ash and Kirsty and asked who they were.

Kirsty had this crazy, starstruck look in her eyes. She said, 'We are Nelson's friends. We wanted to come and experience a truly authentic way of life.'

I turned around and gave her evils while a huge smile spread across Dad's face. He said, 'I am so proud of you, my boy. Recruiting young new adherents to our lifestyle.'

'But Da—'

He cut me off. 'Not now, Nelson. There is much to

show your friends.'

He led the way down the track. Ash and Kirsty were doing silent victory dances. I knew this was going to be horrific.

Over the next couple of hours, Dad gave Ash and Kirsty the grand tour of our manor while I cringed myself into a ball of humiliation.

The worst part was when he tried to hunt a squirrel. He followed it up a tree then lost his grip and fell into a bush.

'OH MY GOD, THAT IS JUST LIKE WHAT HAPPENED IN COUGAR'S VIDEO!' Kirsty yelled.

Dad pulled a bramble out of his beard and said, 'Video? What are you talking about? Who is Cougar?'

I glared at Kirsty and said, 'Nothing. Don't listen to her, she's crazy. She says crazy stuff.'

Afterwards, we built a fire and roasted some of Scarfwick's disgusting fish over it. Dad sat on a tree stump and stroked his beard. You could tell he was loving being a bushcraft guru.

'So tell us more about how we could defend ourselves in the event of an animal attack,' said Ash.

Dad nodded as he chewed on the oily mackerel. He said, 'It is important to make yourself big like a bear.' He hunched his shoulders, held his arms out wide, and roared.

Kirsty and Ash grinned like a pair of morons. This was the worst thing ever. I kept trying to think of a reason to get rid of them but I couldn't come up with anything.

Kirsty leaned in so close, the flames were nearly singeing her eyebrows off. She said, 'And what if that doesn't work?'

'If that doesn't work,' said Dad, 'you should soil yourself.'

Kirsty spluttered with laughter. Dad gave her an evil look so she tried to make it seem like she was coughing.

Ash asked why you had to do that.

Dad said, 'Because the smell may put them off. Failing that, if they do start eating you, they might get to the pooey bit and spit you out. Bears may be ferocious, remorseless killers, but they don't want to eat human waste.'

I face-palmed. Kirsty and Ash had to pretend they were choking to cover their laughs. Mary didn't say much, just kept looking back down the drive towards Primrose's house.

Kirsty was forever coming up with more questions. Stuff like, 'And what about if you're out in nature and you have to dig a toilet trench?'

I eyeballed her as if to say 'shut up' but she ignored me.

Dad said. 'It is important to dig it as far upstream as possible. And remember, if you need to wipe, do not use stinging nettles.'

Kirsty laughed. 'Ah, like you did in that video before!'

Dad stopped smiling. 'What?' He stared at me. 'What is she talking about? What are these videos?'

My heart was kickboxing my ribs. I said, 'Oh, she was talking about me. School had us doing a, um . . . video project about things that interested us, and I did bushcraft. That's how I got them into it.'

Kirsty nodded, obviously sensing an opportunity to dig herself out of the hole. She said, 'Yeah, Ash did one about Superman and I did mine on Midlake Darston.'

Dad wanted to know who that was.

'Oh, he's a YouTube star,' said Kirsty.

Dad growled. 'Do not mention the blasted internet in my house. I will not tolerate talk of so-called YouTube "stars".'

Kirsty giggled and went, 'Ironyyyyyyyy!'

Dad threw his fish bones into the fire and said, 'Nelson, I'm afraid I don't understand what your friend is talking about.'

I threw proper shade at both of them and said to Dad, 'That's OK. I think it's about time they went home, anyway.'

Kirsty huffed. 'But our bus doesn't get here for another fifteen minutes!'

I stood up. 'The buses around here are always early.

Come on.'

'Thank you for having us, Griz—I mean, Mr Lambsley,' Ash said.

Kirsty said, 'Yeah, this has been the BEST.'

Dad was loving it, and was all, 'It is wonderful to see young people so interested in the outdoors. Now all you need to do is spread the word.'

Kirsty was like, 'Oh definitely. I'm going to spread the word to everyone at school.'

Dad stood up and stared into the distance. He had a weird look on his face. A bit like the one when he finally got his organic compost toilet to work. No, I haven't used it. He was like, 'I think you may have given me an idea. Perhaps it is my duty, nay, my calling, to pass my knowledge down to the next generation. Maybe I should visit your school and speak to the children myself. It would earn our way of life a wider audience.'

Kirsty said, 'Oh I don't know, it's pretty wide as it is.'

'If you were a boy, I would punch you,' I muttered.

I walked them down the drive to the bus stop. Once we were far enough away, I let rip. I mean I got annoyed. I didn't fart.

I yelled, 'WHAT THE HELL WAS THAT ALL ABOUT?'

Kirsty was all apologetic, saying stuff like, 'I was just totally overwhelmed. I've never met a celebrity before.'

'And you STILL HAVEN'T,' I said.

She said, 'That's not true. Midlake Darston knows him, and now I know him, so in a way, me and Midlake know each other. This brings me one step closer to my ultimate goal.'

'And what is your ultimate goal?' Ash asked, sighing, as if it was a question he'd asked billions of times before.

Kirsty got this dreamy look in her eyes and said, 'To be Midlake's wife.'

Oh God.

We got to the end of the drive. That crazy bloke from the village went past, singing songs about coal mining on the back of his donkey.

Ash was like, 'Man, do you live in the olden days or what?'

I said, 'Never mind that. What am I supposed to do now? I can't have Dad coming to the school.'

'Aw come on, what's the worst that could happen?' said Kirsty.

I was like, 'People could chant "Grizzly Dadams" at him? The whole thing would be blown? Dad would freak out and kill me? Do you need any more?'

Kirsty said, 'We'll figure something out, tell people they have to be cool. It'll be fine. It has to be. Because if we can get your dad to the school and make a video, Midlake will watch it. And if I get in on the video, he will see me and he will say, "There she is. There is my future wife," and he will fly to England on his private jet and he will come to the school and he will say, "Where is that gorgeous girl from the video?" And I will say, "I'm here, Midlake, I'm here." And he will turn and look at me, and he will bat away all the girls throwing themselves at him like the annoying gnats that they are, and he will say, "There you are, my sweet princess." And he will kiss me, and an orchestra will start playing somewhere.'

There was a pause.

'ARE YOU FINISHED?' I yelled.

Kirsty stopped and grabbed my sleeve. 'Please, Nelson, don't take this away from me. I NEED THIS!'

I said, 'No way.'

She screamed, 'I THOUGHT WE WERE FRIENDS!'

The bus pulled up. I said, 'Oh, here we are, see you guys tomorrow!'

When the bus pulled away, Kirsty was still shouting, 'I NEED THIS!' through the window.

WE ALL HAVE OUR INTERESTS

Kirsty didn't speak to me the next day. It was so weird. She was normally so reasonable, but when it came to that Midlake guy, she had no sense of reality.

She had even changed desks and moved to the back of the room with a murderous expression on her face, carving something into the table top with a compass. I asked Ash why she was being like that.

He said, 'She wants to be seen by Midlake.'

I huffed and slammed my maths book down on the table. 'Then she should make her own videos and get him to watch them.'

Ash said, 'She'd be one in a billion YouTubers desperate for his attention. Grizzly Dadams has a ready-made fan base and Darston is one of them.'

I was like, 'But that's ridiculous. Me getting my mum back is way more important than some pretty boy off the internet catching a glimpse of Kirsty for a split-second.'

Ash looked me right in the eye. I knew he was serious because he never did that. He said, 'You don't get it. I've known Kirsty since we were five. She has been fanatical about him for EVER. Seriously. It's like an obsession. This chance of just being seen by him is a dream come true. Yeah, it's weird, but we all have our interests.' He nodded at his Superman pencil case.

Ugh. I had a horrible feeling he was right. I mean, I know if I had the chance to visit RockWars Studios— the company who make *Streets of Chicago* and *Hip-Hop Zombies*, I would totally lose my mind.

I said, 'OK, fine. I've thought of something that might work.'

I DO PROVIDE MY OWN ACCOMPANIMENT

Mary was confused on the bus home again and asked if Kirsty and Ash lived with us now.

Kirsty leaned forward and wedged her chin in the gap between our headrests. She said, 'I'd love it if we could, Mary, but I think I'd miss TV.'

Mary said, 'We get *Peter the Pirate*, but shhh, Daddy doesn't know about that.'

Dad was delighted that Kirsty and Ash had come back for more lessons. Kirsty was all, 'Ooh, Mr Lambsley, nothing could keep us away. Since the last time I was here, I have thought about NOTHING but bushcraft.'

I muttered, 'All right, dial it down a bit,' then turned to Dad and said, 'I've just got to get something from the outhouse first. Why don't you head inside and get your whittling stuff out?'

Dad's face broke out into a massive grin and he yelled, 'Of course, whittling! The greatest art form known to man.' Then he skipped back into the house.

'If I get caught, I'm blaming it on you,' I said to Kirsty.

179

She gave me a massive hug and yelled, 'You are the BEST.' Then she stepped back and said, 'How do I look?'

Her hair was down, falling over her shoulders instead of up in her usual ponytail. She had put on some of her mum's make-up, too.

I was like, 'Yeah, you look all right.'

She whacked me on the arm and went, 'Ooh, you smooth talker.'

I grumbled and went into the outhouse to grab the camera. Ash had brought one of his old school bags with a camera lens sized hole cut into it. I put the camera in, fit the scope into the hole, and pressed record.

'Here we go,' I said.

When we got inside, Dad was sitting in his whittling chair in front of the fire. He pointed at the rug and went, 'Sit, children, and observe the miracle of creation.'

We did as we were told. Ash wedged a book underneath the bag so it was tilted slightly upwards. Luckily, Dad didn't seem to notice. Kirsty made sure she was sitting in sight of the camera. She kept looking straight at the bag and pouting and I had to subtly poke her leg to get her to stop it.

Dad picked up a block of wood and his whittling knife. He said, 'Now tell me, what would you like me to whittle? I can do anything.'

Ash was like, 'Ah great, how about Superman?'

'Don't be stupid,' said Dad. 'I mean decent things.'

Ash bit his bottom lip. Normally he'd flip his lid at anyone dissing Superman. I reckon the only reason he didn't have a go at Dad was because he would probably fight him like a bear or something.

Kirsty raised her hand and said, 'How about Peter the Pirate?' She winked at Mary, who clapped and cheered.

Dad cut her off, barking, 'NO TELEVISION CHARACTERS.'

Kirsty was like, 'But I thought you said you could whittle anything.'

Dad pinched the bridge of his nose and yelled, 'ANYTHING NATURAL!'

'But Daddy, pirates are natural,' Mary said to him.

Dad dug his whittling knife into the block and grumbled. 'OK, well what do pirates always have?'

Kirsty said, 'Wooden legs? That's a bit easy, to be honest.'

And Ash was like, 'Yeah, I bet even I could whittle one of those.'

'A PARROT,' Dad yelled. 'Pirates have PARROTS.'

He immediately got to work, hacking excess wood away until he had a rough outline.

'Do you have music to listen to while you work?' Kirsty asked.

Dad's brow furrowed. 'I do not have what you might call "popular music" in this house. But I do provide my own accompaniment.'

I face-palmed. Oh God, he was going to sing his whittling song.

Whittling, whittling,
To whittle is the best,
Whittling, whittling,
North, south, east, and west.
Whittling, whittling,
I can whittle anything,
Whittling, whittling,
And when I whittle I sing, sing, sing.

By the time he'd got to the fifteenth verse, everyone was joining in. Except me.

Dad held the finished parrot up to the light and asked for our verdict.

Ash said, 'That is actually excellent.'

'Yeah,' Kirsty said, while tossing her hair around like she was experiencing wild neck spasms. 'That's the best wooden parrot EVER!'

Dad was just starting to apply varnish when a beep cut through the silence. I froze. It was the camera's low battery tone. Oh God, why didn't I charge it?

Dad's eyes shot waves of fury at us. 'What was that noise?'

I said, 'Noise, what noise?' The camera bleeped again and I went, 'Way hay!' to try and cover it.

Dad jabbed a finger at the bag. He said, 'It was coming from in there. It sounded like some kind of electronic device.'

I exchanged a panicked look with Ash. If Dad found that camera, I would be done for.

Ash reached into the front pocket and pulled out his phone. He said, 'Sorry, I thought I'd switched it off.'

Dad growled and said, 'Those devices are banned from this house. I will let you off this once, but if I find any other electronic communication devices in future I will dispose of them. Permanently.'

I waited until Dad was distracted with a new whittling project before I excused myself, took the bag outside, and threw the camera into the hole in the outhouse. That was too close.

* * *

When I walked Kirsty and Ash to the bus stop. Kirsty gave me yet another hug and was all, 'You are the BEST. When I marry Midlake, you can be my maid of honour.' She then patted Ash's shoulder and said, 'Sorry, Ash.'

He was like, 'Oh, I'm sure I'll get over it.'

When they'd gone, I went back to the outhouse and uploaded the whittling video. I edited out the boring bits and by the time I'd finished it was pretty funny. The addition of Kirsty and Ash added an extra layer of comedy which I thought my subscribers would appreciate. As before, I added the picture of Mum to the end. I'd had no tips as yet. No serious ones, anyway.

KRYPTONITE

The next morning, I checked the comments on my latest video. As well as the usual '**LOLs**' and '**GRIZZLY DADAMS ROOLZ**,' there were loads of people asking how they could get hold of some of Dad's ornaments.

Now there was an idea. This internet fame could do wonders for his whittling business. Then, when he had made loads of money, Mum would definitely come back. Between YouTubing and whittling, we could be millionaires!

I wrote the PO Box address Dad put on his whittling adverts in the descriptions of all the videos. Maybe things were on the up after all.

Dad stopped me as Mary and I left for school. He said, 'Oh, let me know if that Tronk fellow says anything to you. I sent him a letter yesterday offering my services.'

NOOOOOOO!

He said, 'Speaking to your school friends has instilled in me a new purpose. I want to spread my message to more young people, and I have offered to visit your school and talk to the children about bushcraft and self-sufficiency.'

Oh no, oh no, oh no. That would be the worst thing ever.

I was like, 'Ohh great. So when did you send it?'

He said, 'Monday night, why do you ask?'

I was all, 'No reason. Just thought I could pop into his office and speak to him—put in a good word.'

Dad put his hand on my shoulder. He said, 'I'm very proud of you, son. You are becoming an excellent advocate for our cause.'

I tried to swallow that heavy guilty feeling in my throat and smile.

After I dropped Mary off, I ran to school and found Ash and Kirsty.

I wiped the sweat from my forehead and said to them, 'You know how I helped you yesterday? Well, now I need you to help me.'

Ash said, 'I don't like the sound of that.'

We went to Mr Tronk's office before the start of form. We knew that he always got his morning cup of coffee from the staffroom before he headed to class, so we were pretty sure it would be empty.

I gave his door a little knock and looked around. There was no 'uh huh' from inside so it looked like it was safe. I tried the handle. Open!

'Right,' I said to Kirsty, 'you're coming in with me to find this letter and Ash can stand guard.'

Kirsty was like, 'Why do I have to go in?' I explained that it was her fault Dad thought he had to go out and spread his message, so she could help me put a stop to it. When I put it like that, she grudgingly agreed.

Ash said, 'Right. Do I need a code word or something?'

I was like, 'A code word? What's that?'

He said, 'You know, in case Tronk comes back and I need to alert you. I could say, like, "Kryptonite" or something.'

Kirsty rolled her eyes and flicked his ear. 'Yeah 'cause that looks totally natural doesn't it? Some gomper standing outside Mr Tronk's office shouting "Kryptonite"?'

'How about you just cough?' I said to Ash.

He shrugged. I turned to Kirsty and nodded. She nodded back and blasted me with what seemed like a sarcastic thumbs up. We took one last look around before we entered.

Sure enough, Tronk's office was just as untidy as last time. He had even left that **KING** light on his shelf switched on. The fish in the dirty bowl below looked kind of old and depressed. There were papers stacked everywhere and his in tray overflowed with opened letters. I had a quick flick through but Dad's wasn't in there.

'He has to keep his mail somewhere,' I whispered to Kirsty. 'Get searching.'

I started on the desk while Kirsty concentrated on his drawers. I mean his desk drawers—he didn't leave his pants lying around.

I began to panic—partly because of the risk of getting caught and partly because I couldn't let him open that letter. I moved Elvis paperweights, old coffee cups, and other junk out of the way but I still couldn't see it. I felt like Reginald Johnson in that bit of *Operation: Nazikiller* when he has to find the key to the jail in the Obergruppenführer's office.

'Any luck over there?' I whispered to Kirsty.

She said, 'Nope. Found the answers to next week's test, though. Just downloading them to the old memory banks.'

I said, 'Never mind that, find the letter!'

I tried the drawer under the desk. YES! It was crammed full of unopened mail. Most of it was catalogues and Elvis Presley fan club newsletters, but then I saw a small, brown envelope with what had to be Dad's scrawly handwriting on it. There was even a massive dirty thumbprint on it.

I held it up and waved it at Kirsty. She jumped and threw her hands in the air, whispering a 'hooray!'

Her left hand hit something on the shelf. The **KING** light. The bulb must have scorched her knuckle because she drew it back and yelped.

But that wasn't the worst.

The light began to topple, as if it was in slow motion. It rocked and wobbled, until finally it fell off the shelf.

Now guys, you're probably thinking, how are they

going to get out of that one? Breaking their teacher's precious **KING** light?

Well, breaking property wasn't the worst thing Kirsty did.

The worst was MURDER.

MURDER

I thought that would be a good place to stop. I really needed a wee. Anyway, I might have exaggerated when I said Kirsty committed murder. It wasn't murder exactly, because it was accidental. It was probably just manslaughter. Or fishslaughter.

You see, the thing is, the **KING** light didn't just fall onto the drawers and break. No, it fell straight into the goldfish bowl.

We screamed as sparks flew and smoke billowed. I jumped across the room and yanked the plug out of the wall. Then I opened the window and tried to waft the smoke out before the alarms went off.

Kirsty covered her eyes with her hands, going, 'OH MY GOD, OH MY GOD, OH MY GOD, HAVE I KILLED IT? HAVE I KILLED THE FISH?'

I fanned more smoke away and peered into the bowl. My stomach churned. It looked like an overdone fish finger.

I was like, 'Um, I think you might have.'

Kirsty screamed again. I put my hand on her shoulder to try and comfort her, but she was having none of it.

'THIS IS THE WORST THING THAT HAS EVER HAPPENED. I AM A MONSTER!'

Her screaming meant I wasn't immediately aware of the office door opening and Mr Tronk standing there with a horrified look on his face. Why didn't Ash warn us?

Tronk said, 'What the devil is goin' on in this place?'

I scratched the back of my head and looked at the ground. This was bad. This was very bad.

I muttered something about wanting to ask him a question about Shakespeare. Tronk didn't have time to poke holes in the logic of that lie because he had already noticed the fish bowl.

He yelled, 'Oh good lawd. The King! The King is dead!'

He whipped his shades off and peeped into the bowl.

He stepped back and shielded his eyes, saying, 'What happened here?'

I stared at Kirsty. She was shaking and her bottom lip wobbled. How were we going to get out of this one?

'I DID IT!' she screamed. 'IT WAS AN ACCIDENT! I KNOCKED YOUR LIGHT OFF THE SHELF AND IT FELL INTO THE BOWL. I'M SO SORRY, MR TRONK, PLEASE DON'T SEND ME TO JAIL!'

She buried her head in his chest and sobbed. Mr Tronk looked at me and raised an eyebrow.

I said, 'It's true. It was an accident.'

Mr Tronk closed his eyes and sighed. He said, 'There, there, little missy. Stop them tears. If I hadn't have left the light on, the King would still be OK.'

'NO!' Kirsty yelled, looking up at him. 'IT WAS MY FAULT! I'M SO SORRY!'

Mr Tronk pulled away and found a box of tissues under all the junk on his desk. Kirsty took one and blew her nose with a loud honk.

'We're going to put this behind us,' said Mr Tronk. 'With a little ceremony.'

* * *

Five minutes later, we were standing in the teachers' toilets. Mr Tronk had put the King in the cleanest one along with some rose petals.

I felt awful. To avoid my mad dad coming to school and blowing everything, I had been an accomplice in the untimely death of a goldfish.

Mr Tronk nodded at the toilet and said, 'So long, little fella. Give my regards to Mama.'

He took a deep breath. Kirsty started snivelling again. Then he started singing. I don't know what song it was, but the first line was, 'Maybe I didn't feed you quite as often as I should have.'

Then he crossed himself and flushed.

'Going out on the toilet,' he said. 'Just like the real King.'

* * *

Anyway, I still feel really bad about this, so this is my confession. I hope, if you've got this far, Mr Tronk, that you understand my reasons for sneaking into your office. Of course, if you don't, you can always put me in detention for the rest of eternity.

Afterwards, with Dad's letter safely torn into billions of tiny pieces, we found Ash and asked him what had happened. Apparently, Marshall Cremaine and his posse had stopped by and started hassling him. He tried to ignore them for a bit, but then Marshall picked him up and started swinging him around. He said he tried to make himself big like my dad said, but it didn't work.

Luckily, Mrs Haskell arrived to put a stop to it before he had to resort to pooing himself.

Normally, Kirsty would have screamed with laughter at something like that, but we were both still too traumatized about the death of the King.

They were serving fish fingers for lunch. Needless to say, we weren't hungry.

MIRACLE

The next morning, Dad slammed a thick bundle of mail down on the table, nearly knocking over my bowl of disgusting porridge.

He was like, 'Just look at all these orders! My whittling business is going supernova. The power of word of mouth.'

More like power of internet, I thought.

I was happy for him—it was good to see his passion paying off, plus the more money we got, the more likely it was that Mum would come back.

But then I stopped. These orders had been sent in by Grizzly Dadams fans. There could be anything written on them. I quickly suggested that I should process them, you know, as a way of learning the family business. Dad was well happy with that, so I picked them up and took them upstairs. When I opened the first few I was relieved—people had filled in the forms as normal—two giraffes, a lion, an oak tree, blah, blah, blah. But a few were clearly people taking the mick. Stuff like 'I LOVE U GRIZZLY DADAMS—I AM A BEAR RARRRR! LOL!' And 'WILL U MARRY ME GRIZZLY? I NO FOR A FACT THAT UR AVAILABLE.'

I sneakily tore the dodgy ones up and came down with the rest.

Dad smiled as he felt the weight of the orders in his hand. Then his smile began to fade. He said, 'Wait, there was more than this.'

I froze. Damn. I hadn't really thought this through. I scratched the back of the head and then forced myself to stop. I always did that when I was lying. Which seemed to be happening a lot.

I said, 'Yeah, the rest was just junk mail. Anyway, come on, Mary, time for school.'

Mary blew a raspberry and jumped out of her chair. We took advantage of the fact that we left a little early to stop by the chicken coop to see Gertrude. Just as we were leaving, Primrose said, 'By the way, if you notice your upload speeds getting quicker soon, it's because the company are installing fibre optic.'

Quicker uploads meant more videos. Things were about to get interesting.

MIDLERRTALKKBAAMAAA

The next few days went the same way—I would sort through the orders as they came in, go to school, come home, stitch together another Grizzly Dadams video, then check for tip-offs about Mum. The only problem was, now Dad had so many orders to get through, he was whittling all the time and not doing as much crazy stuff.

I checked my stats. I was inching ever closer to half a million subscribers. That was a lot of pressure. I was going to have to think of a way of getting Dad to be more Grizzly. My ad money now stood at two hundred quid. Wow. Two hundred. I bet our crummy old house probably cost less than that.

Kirsty still wasn't herself at school, saying she felt like a murderer. It wasn't until lunchtime on Friday that she finally snapped out of it. And in a big way.

She was like, 'OHMYGODOHMYGODOHMYGOD,' and waving her phone.

'What? What is it?' I exchanged a worried glance with Ash. I was beginning to think her nan had died or something like that.

'Midlerrrtalkkbaamaaa,' she blabbered.

I was like, 'Say that again?'

Kirsty grabbed my shoulder. 'Midlerrrsaaamaa.'

It was like she was speaking Martian or something.

'Midlake Darston talked about you?' said Ash.

Wow. I knew they had been friends for years but that was very impressive.

She nodded and shoved her phone in our faces. Sure enough, there was Midlake, chatting on about how funny Grizzly Dadams is and how they should bring back that ginger girl 'cause she is hilarious.

'Hilarrrr,' she rasped. 'Hilarrrr.'

Ash grinned. 'Looks like you're one step closer to that wedding after all.'

Kirsty smiled. Then she picked up her tray, stood up, and fainted.

THE MATING CALL OF THE FOX

The next morning, I got this weird message.

Dear Grizzly Dadams Jr,

Hi, I'm Noah St Claire, CEO of ShockJock Merch, based out of San Diego, Cali. You might know me as the guy who produced the very first LolCat T-shirt. Anyway, the reason I'm getting in touch is, I would love it if you would give us sole rights to the Grizzly Dadams image. We would make tees, hoodies, mugs, you name it.

I stopped reading. No way. Just the videos being out there was bad enough, but having Dad's face on mugs was way too risky. But then, something caught my eye,

We'll offer you $3000 upfront, plus thirty-five cents for every item sold.

Three grand? Three grand? I couldn't agree quickly enough. I mean, would you turn down that much money? I imagined what Mum would say when I told her. She would be so proud of me. Coupled with the money Dad must have been making from the whittling, we were probably rich.

Without properly reading anything, I signed loads of contracts and soon, the money was in my account. Noah offered to send me a box of free Grizzly Dadams merchandise, but I said no. Imagine taking that delivery.

In the meantime, I stepped up the search for Mum, making her photo the channel's profile picture and sending it to all the Grizzly fan pages. Surely someone would know something. Every time I had a new message or notification, my heart would jump, only for it to be someone saying 'LOLZ' or something like that. But still, lying awake at night, listening to Dad outside trying to imitate the mating call of the fox in order to lure one out of its hiding place, I had to believe that it was only a matter of time.

INTERNET PEOPLE

After fainting in the dinner hall, Kirsty was kept off school. It was probably just as well because if she wasn't, she'd have bullied me into making another video. And she'd have been so desperate for more attention from Midlake that she would have definitely given us away.

The next morning, I set about making a new Grizzly Dadams video. This one would have to be spectacular if it was going to please all of my subscribers. Problem was, I had no ideas. Dad was mainly whittling in his little nook by the window, and I couldn't think of a way of getting him out. I needed inspiration.

I decided to take a walk down to the harbour. Mr and Mrs Scarfwick were outside the hut having an argument. I won't describe word-for-word what it sounded like but imagine there's a factory where they make swear words. Now imagine it has exploded. That's what it sounded like.

Mr Scarfwick was waving at a broken-down old boat on a trailer. 'It's fixable,' he kept saying.

Mrs Scarfwick was having none of it and insisted that he had to get rid. She was like, 'Burn it, smash it to pieces, I don't care. Just get shot of it. I won't have you cluttering our yard with any more of your junk.'

I was about to walk away, but then I stopped. This could have been just the thing I was looking for.

I said, 'Hey, if you don't want the boat, we'll take it off your hands. We'll always need firewood.'

Mr Scarfwick went to protest, but his wife screeched, 'It's yours,' then fell asleep standing up.

I went up and told Dad that the Scarfwicks were giving away a free boat. Needless to say, he was pretty keen on the idea—especially since reading the latest Blimmington-Weltby book—*Fishing Your Way to Self Sufficiency*. The front cover is Panther punching a shark in the face.

Dad was all, 'Think of it, son. With our new vessel, we can catch our own fish and discover uncharted waters.'

I chuckled to myself. The only uncharted waters that thing was going to discover were at the bottom of the sea.

We went back down in the car and towed the boat up the hill. Mary kept calling it the *Jolly Polly*, after Peter the Pirate's boat. I'm pretty sure Peter the Pirate's boat didn't have big chunks missing, but I wasn't going to spoil it for her.

While Dad prepared his tools, I hid the camera in a hedge.

Dad laid some lengths of wood on the floor and took out his hammer. He said, 'It is time to begin. Soon, we will

RULE THE WAVES!'

He hammered one of the new pieces of wood in, which made one of the old pieces fall out. He tried again and the same thing happened. Then some of the new ones started to come out because the wood at the end was so rotten.

Dad growled and whacked a nail back in. Unfortunately, he forgot to move his thumb.

He was like, 'YOOOOOOOWWWW! This damned boat!' Then he let rip with a string of words that made Scarfwick sound like a choirboy. I covered Mary's ears and tried not to laugh. This was going to be another great video.

I heard a car approach from down the lane. My heart skipped. Every time I heard tyres I thought it would be Mum coming to get us. I got up to investigate. The car had to stop because of the massive pile of wood from the boat blocking the road.

Three men got out of the car. One of them had a camera around his neck. I had a bad feeling about this. I went up to them and said, 'Everything OK?'

'It's him, you know,' one said to the other.

'Nah, it ain't,' said the other.

The camera bloke got his phone out, squinted at it, then at me.

'You're right, Phil. It is him.'

I was like, 'What are you talking about?'

The one called Phil said, 'We're from the *Daily Echo*

and we have reason to believe that this is the home of internet sensation, Grizzly Dadams.'

NO! NO! NO! I turned around. Dad was lying down, trying to fix the bottom of the boat. I told them they were wrong.

They chuckled. 'That's funny, because you look just like his kid, Cougar.'

I told them it was a coincidence and that they should leave our property immediately. They didn't move. I thought about making myself big, like a bear, but come on, that wasn't going to work in real life, was it?

Suddenly, the camera guy pointed down the drive and said, 'Wait a minute, lads. There he is!'

I turned and looked towards the house. Dad had got to his feet and was kicking Scarfwick's boat.

I turned and ran back up the drive. The men followed.

Dad glared at them and was like, 'What's happening, Nelson? Who are those men?'

I tried to suck some oxygen back into my lungs. This is it, I thought. Game over. I'm done for. There was no way I could get rid of them without them blabbing. Unless . . .

'They're . . . internet people,' I said to Dad. 'They're trying to force us to get internet!'

Dad's eyes went huge. He picked up his hammer and strode towards them.

One of them shouted, 'Hey, Grizzly Dadams, it's great

to see you!'

Dad gave me a look, then turned back to them. He said, 'Are you internet people?'

The two men shared a glance that was both panicked and confused.

Dad threw his head back, screamed, and chased them back down the drive with his hammer. They leapt back into the car. Dad dived onto the bonnet and stared in through the window. He screamed, 'Take your internet and shove it, you DISGUSTING CREATURES.'

Without thinking, I grabbed Mary and ducked around the back of the outdoor toilet. I mean, I knew Dad was kind of mad, but that was the first time I had seen him lose it in such a horrible way. I felt like I was vibrating with sheer panic, but I did my best to convince Mary that Daddy was only playing.

When Dad found us, he seemed to have calmed down, even though he was still sweating and had flecks of spit in his beard. He said, 'Sorry about that, but you know how I feel about the internet. Still, I wonder why they called me that odd name.'

My heart pounded, my mouth went bone dry. I tried to act casual, all 'What odd name?'

'Grizzly something,' Dad said.

I said I didn't know and suggested that maybe it was because of how bear-like he made himself.

Dad hesitated, then nodded as if that made perfect sense.

WHAT WOULD GRIZZLY DADAMS DO?

As well as everything else, my hair was beginning to annoy me. My fringe was getting in my eyes and everything. It had been months since my last cut. Mum's a hairdresser, so she used to do it for me.

I found Dad in the kitchen. He was reading a book called *To Kill a Mockingbird* and moaning because it had no practical instructions.

I said, 'Dad, can I have some money to go and get a haircut after school?'

Yes, I know I had loads of money, but he didn't know that, did he?

Dad threw the book down and looked up at me. He said, 'Nelson, my boy, have you learned nothing since we've been here?'

I've learned that you're stone cold crazy, I thought.

He went on without me having to answer. He said, 'We are now completely self-sufficient. And that includes haircuts.'

He went to the cupboard and pulled out a bowl and

a pair of scissors he had sharpened on a stone. He was going to stick that on my head and snip around it. I have never run so fast in my life.

The next morning, I met Kirsty and Ash at the bus stop. When we got to the gates, there was a gang of people with iPads and cameras. This was nothing new. Kids had been not-so-secretly filming me at school since Dad became famous, but this was different. These people looked like they might be a real problem. One of them squinted at me and said, 'There he is!'

Kirsty, Ash, and I found ourselves surrounded. They were all shouting at me, wanting to know where they could find Dad. I tried to push my way past, but there were too many of them. Ash held his bag in front of his face and Kirsty was all, 'BACK OFF, YOU PIGS, HE DOESN'T WANT TO TALK TO YOU. AND ALSO, MIDLAKE, IF YOU'RE WATCHING THIS, I LOVE YOU, AND I LIVE AT NUMBER FIFTY-FIVE, DUKES ROAD, SNESSPORT, NR6 7—'

Before she could finish, the reporters parted as someone pushed their way into the scrum. I recognized his voice before he appeared.

'What in the good Lord's name is going on here?'

Mr Tronk stood in front of us. The back of his leather jacket had 'KING' written in sparkly diamonds.

One of the reporters said, 'We're looking for Grizzly Dadams. Do you know him?'

They all shouted over the top of each other, but Tronk silenced them with a raised hand, just like he does in class. He said, 'I don't know no Grizzly Dadams, but what I do know is you fellers look like you're here for a show.'

Before they could say anything, he whipped a comb out of his back pocket, held it up to his mouth like a microphone, and started singing. The reporters carried on filming. I'm sure I heard one of them say something like, 'Are all the adults this kid knows insane?'

With the spotlight off me, the three of us were able to sneak away. I was relieved to have escaped, but now they'd tracked me down to school, it was surely only a matter of time before they got to Dad.

We decided to avoid the main gate and cut through the little path that led around the back of the field. The horrible green brook flanked it the whole way. It was so stinky, I almost gagged. We reached the corner of the field, near the cut through, when a massive shadow stepped out in front of us. Marshall Cremaine. He must have been hiding in the bushes.

He said, 'Bet you're wondering how them journalisms knew you were here.'

I shrugged and said, 'I figured they just followed my bus or something.'

He growled and said, 'It was me. I told them.'

Kirsty growled right back and said to him, 'Why would

you do that?'

Marshall was all, 'Because I always win, you bunch of freaks. Do you know how embarrassed I was that that stupid greasy teacher stopped me before I could smash your face in?'

I laughed and said, 'I'm pretty sure I was winning.'

Marshall grunted and shoved me. I stumbled back into the metal fence.

Ash jumped forward and yelled, 'Hey, don't touch him.'

Marshall said, 'When did you grow a backbone, squirt? How's about I send you for another Dip so you know your place?'

Ash puffed out his chest. 'I am no squirt,' he said. 'I am the Man of Steel.'

I know. Amazing.

Marshall folded his arms. 'Superman sucks. Everyone knows the Hulk is the best superhero.'

Ash said, 'You would say that. Who are you, his stupider younger brother?'

Kirsty laughed and high fived Ash. 'Good one, mate,' she said.

Marshall turned to Kirsty and huffed out of his nose like a bull who'd just spotted a red rag. He said, 'I saw you on that video, freak. I don't know why you're so obsessed with that Midlake loser. He's a wimp.'

Kirsty squared up to Marshall and said, 'Take that back.'

Marshall chuckled and rubbed his zitty chin. 'And I'll tell you something else, he ain't even good-looking.'

Kirsty said, 'Take that back,' again, this time sounding threatening.

'In fact,' Marshall went on, 'I reckon he's proper ugly.'

Kirsty turned her head quick and waggled her eyebrows at Ash. Ash nodded and slid past me so he was out of Marshall's eyeline. Marshall advanced on Kirsty, pushing her closer to the fence, taunting her about Midlake. I watched in a mixture of amazement and horror as Ash got down on his hands and knees behind Marshall's legs. He coughed quickly and nodded. I looked up at Kirsty, who by now had a big smile on her face. She said, 'Nothing you can say will make me change my mind about Midlake. I will always watch his videos. In fact, I think tonight I'm going to watch fifty of them.'

Marshall laughed and said, 'Saddo.'

'Yep,' Kirsty said, ignoring him. 'I'm going to settle down on the settee with a bag of Doritos and a massive jar of . . . DIP!'

She shoved Marshall, making him fall backwards over Ash and land in the disgusting green brook with an enormous splash.

He stood up, dry heaving and swearing, trying to climb

out, but finding the bank too slippery.

I said, 'Wow, he really does look like the Hulk now.'

Kirsty cackled, took a photo on her phone, and then ran through the gap in the fence. Me and Ash followed before we got Hulk-smashed.

When we were a safe distance away, I clapped Ash on the back. I said, 'Thanks for sticking up for me, mate.'

Kirsty agreed. 'Yeah, man. What got into you?'

Ash smiled to himself and looked at the floor. He said, 'I think it's spending time with your dad.'

I know, guys. I know. I was like, 'Are you serious?'

He nodded and said, 'I found myself thinking—what would Grizzly Dadams do?'

Kirsty honked with laughter and said, 'You should totally get that bloke to print that on a T-shirt.'

MESSAGE

When we got home that afternoon, I noticed a bike propped up against the wall. I knew it couldn't have been Mum. I mean, why would she turn up on a BMX? I followed the sound of Dad's voice around the back and saw him talking to this bloke I'd never seen before. He was wearing similar clothes to Dad—old baggy T-shirt, khaki trousers, sandals, and a huge, floppy hat. Dad was telling him about how he was planning to make his own toilet paper, when he spotted me and Mary.

He was all, 'Children! So glad you're home. This is Scott. He just happened to be passing by and saw me whittling outside. He is interested in our way of life!'

This Scott looked at me with a weird expression in his face. I glanced at his hat and noticed a tiny black dot in the centre of it. Almost like a hidden camera. I folded my arms and stared him out.

Scott said, 'Yes, it has been very . . . interesting. But now I must go.'

Dad tried to protest and said, 'You mean you're not staying for dinner? I'm cooking my freshly caught fish stew. I buy it from a local tradesman, but soon I will have my own vessel.' He nodded at the pile of firewood that used to be a boat in the corner. I noticed Scott's mouth twitch upwards—he would have seen the video where Dad was trying to fix that.

'Don't try and force him to stay,' I said to Dad, never taking my eyes off this Scott's face. 'I mean, he's obviously got somewhere to be.'

Scott murmured some thanks to Dad, then got back on his bike and left, probably nervous that I was going to blow his cover.

A couple of days later, I was in the middle of yet another attempt to find Mum online when I saw something pop up on Google.

My Day with Internet Sensation, Grizzly Dadams—a special undercover report by Byron Hinchcliffe.

I felt sick. The article wasn't lies exactly, but it had this way of exaggerating the truth. It said stuff about Dad having a 'shrine to Panther Blimmington-Weltby,' when actually, it was just a shelf with his books on. And a framed photo. I had to stop reading about halfway down. Dad was being targeted by people and it was all my fault. It would be only a matter of time before he found out how famous he was and I didn't know how much longer I was going to be able to keep it from him. At one point, he even offered to take us for a ride into Hemlington, the nearest big town, and I had to pretend to be ill to stop him. Imagine if we'd have gone—he might have got mobbed.

Something had to happen—and soon. Before I shut the computer down, I checked my YouTube account again. I had a few messages. They were mostly spam, or trolls, but then I got to one from this bloke called Roger Norbert. It said,

> ***I know where your Mum is.*** ✉

WHAT IS THE MEANING OF THIS?

To begin with, I thought it was another joke. There was a link at the bottom, which was always a dead giveaway. I ran it through the virus scanner and it came back clean.

It was a site for a newspaper called the *Grundsford Herald*. I knew Grundsford. It was about a ten-minute drive from our old house.

The headline on the page said, 'New Salon Opens in Town.'

OK, I thought. Mum used to be a hairdresser, but that doesn't mean . . .

I scrolled down. When I saw her smiling face, I burst into tears straight away.

She was standing in front of some mirrors in a salon with three women and a man. She had got a job. Probably to get more money. When she found out how much I made from YouTubing, she would be overjoyed.

I wiped my eyes with the sleeve of my hoodie and ran out of the outhouse. I had to tell Mary and Primrose.

Mary skipped on the spot when I told her. She was

like, 'You mean Mummy is coming back? I am going to give her a MASSIVE kiss!'

I shushed her as we approached Primrose's house. I could hear voices. I thought it was more reporters. I crept through the trees and ducked behind a bush. Peering out, I could make out two men with their backs to me, installing a big metal box at the end of the drive. They were both wearing florescent vests with 'Fibre Optic Broadband' printed on them.

Ah. This time it really was internet people.

I knocked on Primrose's door. When she answered, that sweet cooking smell wafted out. She thought we'd come to see Gertrude. When I told her that one of the Grizzly Dadams fans had tipped us off about Mum's whereabouts, she punched the air, then scooped us both up in a big hug.

I said I didn't really know what to do. Should I call the shop? Primrose said we should tell Dad. Before I could question whether that was a good idea, I was stopped by a roar. An actual roar. It was like when Dad was being a bear but a lot louder. And angrier.

Dad ran down the drive and stood in the middle of Primrose's flower bed. He screamed, 'WHAT IS THE MEANING OF THIS?'

In one hand was the camera. In the other was the laptop.

It was happening. The nightmare was coming true. My heart pounded like mad, and I got that hot feeling in the back of my head—you know the one you get when you are proper panicking. I tried to say something, conjure up some kind of lie, but I had nothing.

Dad stomped closer to us and held the stuff up high.

He shouted, 'Where did you get these? Did she give them to you?'

I shook my head and attempted to get some words out of my stupid mouth.

Primrose put her hand on my shoulder and said, 'It's OK, Nelson. Actually, I did.'

Dad looked like he was about to explode.

Primrose stepped closer to Dad. She said to him, 'Look, I don't want to tell you how to raise your children, but surely they need to be able to do normal kid stuff. I mean, how do you expect them to do homework?'

Dad huffed and said, 'They can consult my array of encyclopaedias.'

I said, 'Dad, your array of encyclopaedias is five Panther Blimmington-Weltby books.'

He turned to me and yelled, 'WHAT ELSE DO YOU NEED? I moved you out here to get you away from poisonous technology and all the while, you were betraying me?'

Tears started brimming in my eyes. He was right, I was betraying him. But he didn't know the worst of it. Yet.

The first thing he noticed was Gertrude, pecking at some seeds on the floor. His eyes went huge and he was all, 'And it seems my neighbour is a thief after all! You have taken food out of the mouths of my children!'

I was about to interrupt and tell him that it was me and Mary who took the chicken, but then he spotted the other thing. The fibre-optic fitters.

He said, 'What is this? More internet men coming to force that foul filth upon my family? NOT WHILE THERE IS BREATH IN MY BODY!'

He ran at the fibre-optic men, screaming like a bear. They turned around. First, they looked terrified. Then they started laughing. The one bloke was like, 'Oh my God, it's Grizzly Dadams!'

I covered my face. This could not be happening.

Dad growled. 'What is it with you internet people calling me that?'

'Ah, mate,' the other man said. 'This bloke is your biggest fan. He's always watching your videos.'

Dad looked all around, confusion and anger plastered across his face. He was all, 'Videos? What videos?'

Primrose gave us a look and approached Dad. I think she was going to try and calm him down. I didn't know what to do. I held Mary's hand.

The internet bloke chuckled and said, 'You really don't know? Check this out.'

He unzipped his fluorescent vest and showed him his T-shirt. I nearly fainted.

On it was a cartoon of Dad, with GRIZZLY DADAMS above it in big red letters. He had a speech bubble coming from his mouth saying, 'I AM A BEAR!'

I knew that merchandise deal would come back to haunt me.

I grabbed Mary's hand and whispered to her, 'That's it, we're going.'

She said, 'Going where?'

'To find Mum,' I said.

Making sure Dad and Primrose were still distracted by the internet people, I dragged Mary towards the woods at the end of the drive.

She put the brakes on, digging her heels into the dirt. She cried out, 'Wait! We can't go without Gertrude. Daddy said he was going to eat her!'

I quickly grabbed Gertrude, picked up a straw bag, emptied the carrots out of it, and put her inside. Then, we took off through the trees.

I thanked the King in fishy heaven that the bus was at the stop at the end of the drive. We jumped on and with a flash of our pass, we were away.

Mary looked up at me and said, 'How are we going to find Mummy, Nelson?'

I didn't know what to say. I mean, I knew where she worked but had no idea how we were going to get there. This bus was going to Snessport. I knew there was a big station there that probably had buses to Norwich. After that, I didn't know what we would do.

The bus was full and people kept giving us odd looks

when our bag started clucking. I glanced at my watch. Five o'clock. Gertrude's usual feeding time. Mary reached into her little bag and pulled out a handful of grain. At least the chicken wasn't going hungry. I dug into my pocket. I had twenty-five pounds. That had to get us all the way up to Grundsford.

When we got off the bus at Snessport, my brain whizzed like a windmill. I didn't know if we were doing the right thing—I just knew I couldn't face Dad's fury now he knew about Grizzly Dadams. Once we found Mum, she could talk him down and get him to shave his beard off and throw out the Panther Blimmington-Weltby books and we could become a normal family again. She was good at stuff like that. I remember when I was little, I was convinced that there was a monster living under my bed and it was only Mum that could calm me down and get me off to sleep.

I looked down at Mary, hand-feeding Gertrude and humming the *Peter the Pirate* theme. She didn't seem worried at all. I suppose to her, we were just going to see Mummy.

The sun started to set. Mary shivered. I gave her my coat as we walked to the bus station. The bottom dragged along the floor like a cape.

All the way there, I kept looking around. I thought that if Dad was going to come looking for us, this was the first place he would try. Every time a car went past, I would look away, searching for an escape route in case it was Dad coming after us.

The bus station was cold and depressing—all bare concrete and overflowing bins. We walked over to the departures board. The furthest away we could get was Norwich and that was leaving in five minutes. Luckily, my bus pass was fully paid up and under-sixes and chickens went free.

Mary got comfy in her seat but there was no way I could relax. I had never run away from home before. I knew Dad would have been worrying about us, but I was going to get in touch as soon as we got to Mum's.

As the bus pulled out of the station, a heavy feeling filled my stomach. This was really happening. I thought maybe I should have stayed and explained that I was only doing it to get our family back together. He would have understood, wouldn't he? But then I remembered how angry he was. What if he went full-on Shining?

The journey to Norwich seemed to take forever. I couldn't make my mind up all the way there. Part of me wanted to get off and call Dad, but another part wanted to see it through. I focused on Mum. She probably had a lovely warm bed in a house with carpets and central heating and indoor toilets and TV.

I tried to think about that—to concentrate on nice

stuff—the four of us back together again in our old house. I closed my eyes and we were there—it was Christmas Day. Mum and Dad sat together on the settee in their dressing gowns, tired and smiling while me and Mary opened our presents. The smell of turkey drifting out of the kitchen while those cheesy songs play softly in the background. It was proper magical.

Then I opened my eyes, saw Norwich, and the magic evaporated.

NORWICH

After checking a wall map that told us how to get to the train station, we headed out into the cold night. It was completely dark and the wind had a nasty bite to it.

Now, I know this might make me sound like a wuss, but Norwich on a Saturday night is terrifying. It was full of people dressed in weird outfits swearing worse than Scarfwick. Even Gertrude seemed a bit spooked. I think all the fried chicken places must have been freaking her out.

I walked as quick as I could, but Mary started to complain that she was getting a stitch so I had to slow down.

I guided us towards the station, following the little black signs and trying to avoid eye contact with all the mad people stumbling past. Smells invaded my nostrils from every doorway—sweet and sour pork, greasy chips, kebabs.

I looked down at Mary, expecting her to be petrified. She wasn't. She was singing to Gertrude.

The station was like an oasis of normality. Yeah, there

was still the odd weirdo, but they were dotted around and didn't seem quite so intimidating. The station was brightly lit and shops I remembered from when we lived in civilization waited for us like old friends. Ah, WH Smiths, Burger King, Claire's Accessories, I have missed you SOOO much.

Actually, I didn't really miss Claire's Accessories, but you get the idea.

We headed over to the ticket area. A security guard looked at us weird. I don't know if it was because we were two kids on our own or whether it was because we had a chicken in a bag, but I wasn't about to stick around to find out. We ducked behind a pillar where the self-service machines were.

There were no direct trains to Grundsford. We had to get one to Birmingham New Street and catch the local service from there. I pressed the button for a child's ticket. Then I had to pick my eyes up off the floor.

SEVENTY QUID.

SEVENTY. QUID.

Right, now I know this channel has got a few subscribers but I doubt the Prime Minister is one of them. Even so, if anyone listening to this is mates with him, have a word because that is a liberty. How do they expect anyone to get anywhere?

I knew there was no way we'd be able to afford that, so

we were going to have to take a risk.

Mary rubbed her eyes and asked me what we were doing.

'We're sneaking onto the train,' I said.

She looked confused and said, 'But isn't that naughty?'

I looked at the ceiling, trying to think of a way to explain it to her. There was literally an army of pigeons up there. I said, 'Yeah, it kind of is, and normally we wouldn't do it, but this is our secret mission, remember?'

I'm so glad I made up that secret mission thing. Works every time.

DODGY CURRY

The 19.05 service to Birmingham New Street pulled into the station. Apparently it was 'comprised of four carriages' and there were no refreshments because of a mix-up in Lowestoft. Weird, the things you remember, isn't it?

Every inch of my skin prickled as we jumped over the gap onto the train. All the other passengers seemed too busy or tired to care about what we were doing, but even so, I was nervous. I picked some seats near the doors. Mary sat down and started fussing over Gertrude. She asked me if she could take her out for a while. I said no.

'Why?' she said.

I said, 'Because you're not supposed to take chickens on trains.'

'Why?'

The doors of the train closed and we slowly pulled out of the station.

'Just because.'

'Why?'

I scrunched my face up. I really didn't have an answer for her. I said, 'Because they all look the same and loads of them would be able to travel using the same pass.'

A man on the other side of the aisle with his finger knuckle-deep in his nose gave us a funny look. I leaned forward to block his view.

'Look,' I whispered to Mary, 'I promise that we can let her out when we get to Mummy's, OK?'

Mary huffed then nodded. 'OK.'

We went quiet for a while. I kept turning around in my seat looking out for the conductor. There was no sign of one. Yet.

'Nelson?' Mary said.

'What is it, Mary?' I replied, still scanning the carriage.

'Is Mummy going to be happy to see us?'

I asked her what she meant.

She shrugged and said, 'It's just, if she went away from us, maybe she doesn't like us any more.'

Oh man. What do you say to that? Her eyes went all teary and I had a lump in my throat the size of a boulder. There's no way I could have both of us crying on a train in front of a load of strangers. They'd definitely know something was up. The nose-picking man was still staring at us.

I said, 'Of course she likes us,' and put my hand on her shoulder. 'She loves us, you silly flump.'

Mary rubbed her eyes and asked, 'Then why did she go?'

I looked around the carriage again and said, 'I don't know, maybe she just needed a little bit of time away. I bet looking after us made her tired, that's all.'

Mary's chin stopped wobbling. Disaster averted.

'Hey, kid.'

For about a second. I turned around and looked at the man across the aisle.

'Are you two on your own?' he asked.

'No,' Mary said. 'We have Gertrude.'

I shot her a quick look. The man looked confused. I said to him, 'Gertrude is our aunt.'

He was like, 'Yeah? And where is she?'

'In the, um . . . toilet!' I said. 'Yeah, she's been in there since we left. Dodgy curry.'

The man nodded and went back to his paper, not looking completely convinced.

I glanced at my watch. We had only been on the train for ten minutes—we had three more hours of this. I didn't know if I could cope. Outside, flat, black fields rolled by, with the occasional sprinkling of lights from a faraway village. I felt my eyes begin to close.

NO! Stay awake. Falling asleep is how you get caught. I thought about the house—about what Dad would do without us. I thought about school. What would Ash and Kirsty say when I didn't show up on Monday? Was Marshall going to hunt them down?

I realized then how much I was going to miss them. Sure, we could Skype each other, but it wouldn't be the same. Looking at one of Ash's Superman doodles over a webcam wouldn't be as good, and there is nothing that could replicate Kirsty's arm punches. In a weird way, I'd even miss Mr Tronk. I mean, yeah, there are teachers in every school, but he is by far the weirdest. Speaking of which, I glanced at an iPad over the shoulder of a woman sitting in the seat next to us. She was on Facebook watching a video of Tronk performing for the press.

I began to think that I was making a big mistake.

I was considering getting off the train at the next stop when a voice at the other end of the carriage jolted me out of my thoughts.

'Tickets, please.'

FIRST CLARSE

Where did he come from? I poked Mary's arm and she was all, 'Ow, what did you do that for?'

I said, 'We've got to move,' never taking my eyes off the conductor. He was an overweight man who looked about sixty, so I thought we could outrun him.

Mary asked why. AGAIN.

The nose picker looked over at us. I pretended not to notice him.

'Because Aunt Gertrude has our tickets and we need to go and get them.'

'But Gertrude is in my ba—'

I pulled her up by her arm and bashed the door open button. We moved quickly into the other carriage. I peered through the window and saw nose picker talking to the conductor and pointing our way. I muttered a Scarfwick-level swear word and dragged Mary along the aisle, not caring whose legs I kicked on the way. I saw a sign up ahead. TOILET. Ah yes. We could hide in there until Birmingham. It would be smelly but it would be safe.

As we reached the head of the carriage, the door at

the other end opened. That conductor really was after us. I smashed the toilet's open button. Nothing. Someone must have been in there.

'Excuse me,' the conductor called over to us. 'Young man, I need to see your tickets.'

I ducked around the corner. The conductor called after us again, this time sounding angrier. We had nowhere to go. If we carried on, he would find us.

Mary said, 'Nelson, I'm scared.'

I didn't want to admit I was too.

The footsteps got closer.

That was when I noticed the cases. Someone had left a pile of them near the doors. I pulled Mary behind me and curled into a ball. The footsteps drew closer still until the conductor was standing right next to us. He hammered on the toilet door.

'Come out, I need to see your ticket.'

'Can it wait, love?' replied what sounded like an old lady. 'I had a couple of glasses of wine at dinner and they've gone straight through me.'

The conductor said, 'Never mind', and carried on. My heart beat faster than the train. I held my breath. He hit the button and entered the next carriage.

'Has he gone?' said Mary. 'Can we come out?'

I whispered, 'No. He'll be back soon. We have to wait for him to go back to his little room at the back.'

She said, 'I don't like this, Nelson.'

'I know,' I replied. 'But it's our secret mission, remember?'

Mary hugged her knees, pouted, and said, 'I hate the secret mission.'

After what felt like five years, but was probably five minutes, the conductor came back through the doors, walking right past us back the way he came.

Mary wanted to move because her legs hurt but I wouldn't let her. We had no choice but to hide there until we got to Birmingham.

An announcement came over the tannoy, saying, 'Next stop: Dereham. Please take all your personal belongings with you, blah, blah, blah.'

The train slowed to a halt. The brakes were proper squeaky which meant I didn't hear the footsteps approaching.

The nose picker lifted off the top case and looked down at us. You should have seen his face, it was like, 'YEAH, VICTORY!' He said, 'Ah, so there you are, thought you could hide, did you?'

I said, 'No. We just prefer sitting on the floor, that's all.'

The man picked up his suitcases as the doors opened. 'I hope you haven't been rooting through my bags.'

I said, 'Hope you haven't been rooting through your nose!'

He huffed and went, 'That's it, I'm getting the conductor.'

I said, 'Fine. If you want to miss your stop, be my guest.'

The man grumbled, shook his head, and jogged off the train just before the doors closed.

The tannoy crackled again. 'Welcome aboard the 19:55 service to Birmingham New Street. A ticket inspector will be passing through the train shortly so would any passengers joining us at Dereham—and any others I may have missed—please have their tickets ready for inspection.'

I jumped to my feet and peeped around the corner—the old lady had come out of the toilet. I said, 'Quick, Mary. Get up.'

'But you said we were staying here,' she said.

'Yes, but that was before that man took his cases away. I've found us another hiding place.'

Mary struggled to her feet and tottered over to me—the movement of the train making her lose her balance slightly. I looked around the corner and saw the toilet door open and a man walk in. He was carrying a newspaper.

I groaned, 'Ugh, he's going to be in there for ages. Come on, we have to find somewhere else.'

I turned around and headed towards the next carriage, Mary followed slowly. I offered to carry Gertrude but Mary was all, 'NO, she's MY chicken.'

I pressed the door open button
and ushered Mary and Gertrude into
the bit that joins carriages—where it's
really loud and the floor moves like you're in a
funhouse. I turned around and saw the conductor at
the end of the other carriage, checking people's tickets. I
smashed the other button and moved on quickly.

'Where are we going to go, Nelson?' Mary yelled.

A woman in the seat next to us shot us some evils and
shushed. Turns out we were in the 'quiet carriage'.

'Keep walking,' I whispered. 'We'll get off at the next
station and catch the next train. Hopefully that one won't
have a conductor.'

I glanced up at the rail map on the wall. The next stop
was Kings Lynn. It looked far away. This was going to be
difficult.

When we reached the head of the carriage by the doors,
there was nowhere to hide. The conductor appeared at the
other end. I squeezed Mary's hand and led her through
another moving compartment into the next carriage. This
one looked different to all the others. The chairs were nicer
and the people looked a bit posher.

'Excuse mehhh,' said this old lady in a pair of half-
moon glasses. 'Do you have first clarse tickets?'

We stopped. 'Um, are you some kind of first class

conductor?' I asked her.

She scowled at me as if she had just bit down on a slice of lemon. 'No.'

'All right, then,' I said and carried on. I'd only been in first class for ten seconds but I hated it already. I mean, if it was seventy quid for a normal child's ticket, how much must she have paid? If it goes up according to how old you are—a million pounds, probably.

I heard the door open behind us and picked up the pace, dragging Mary behind me.

'Excuse me, conductahh?' I heard the old woman's annoying voice. 'Some children came through hyahh and I don't think they had first clarse tickets.'

He said, 'Yes, I've been looking for them since Norwich. Which way did they go?' He sounded proper out of breath.

'They went that way,' said the old woman.

I looked around. Ahead of us was a heavy-looking door with a 'keep out' sign on it. It must have been where the driver sat. To the side of us was the snack shop, empty because of the Lowestoft cock-up.

I swallowed hard and grabbed the Gertrude bag. Then I lifted Mary over the serving hatch and plonked her behind the counter.

I told her to hide as I grabbed the bag and hopped over.

The conductor stomped into the room. I could hear

his heavy breathing. He probably wasn't used to running around after kids. He grumbled something under his breath, then unlocked the driver's door and went inside.

I said to Mary, 'Come on. We're going back the other way.'

Mary grunted in frustration. 'I don't want to. I'm tired. I want to go to bed.'

I pulled her up, shoved her over the counter, and followed, holding onto the bag.

I hurried her along the aisle. All the poshoes looked at us weird.

'How did you . . . ?' The snooty old lady stood up and blocked our way, looking like she'd just had her handbag nicked. 'I sent the conductahh that way.'

I was like, 'Look, we don't have a first class ticket and now we're leaving first class, what's the problem?'

She huffed out through her nose and was like, 'The conductahh said he was looking for you. I think you're a couple of grotty little fare dodgers, aren't you?'

Blood rushed to my face. I said, 'Hey, we're not grotty.'

She was all, 'You certainly look it. And what is that smell?' She peered down at the bag through her little glasses. 'Good lord, is that a—'

'GET HER, GERTRUDE,' Mary yelled as she reached in, grabbed the chicken, and threw it at the old woman.

And that was when things went downhill. Fast.

WHAT'S YOUR STORY, THEN?

There was a security guard waiting for us on the platform at Kings Lynn. He looked even less friendly than the conductor—and trust me, he was NOT friendly.

I don't know if you've ever seen a mad chicken set loose in a first class train carriage, but it was not a pretty sight. Gertrude had been cramped in that bag for hours and she was hungry for freedom. She flapped around the carriage clucking, pooing, and helping herself to bits of people's sandwiches. You should have seen it, guys. It was proper carnage. All the posh people were yelling and swatting at Gertrude with rolled up newspapers. Mary chased after her, climbing over seats and leaving dirty footprints everywhere. That old lady that was trying to block us stomped over to the wall with a mouthful of feathers and pressed the emergency button. The train came to a stop and the conductor found us. We were guilty of fare-dodging and bringing a live chicken on board— both of which were punishable by massive fines. Once he found out that we were travelling on our own, he called ahead to Kings Lynn and told them to have security ready.

The guard led us along the platform until we came to a grey door. He pulled out a huge set of keys, picked one out, and opened the door with it. He raised his eyebrows at us and pointed into the room.

I thought about making a run for it. I could probably make it. But Mary couldn't. And anyway, even if she could, where would we go? We don't know anyone in Kings Lynn. I didn't even know it was a real place until the train got there.

I sighed and walked in, holding Mary's hand. I was relieved to find that it wasn't a jail cell or a torture dungeon or anything like that. It was a normal office with a desk and a couple of chairs. The guard told us to sit down. We did as we were told. I held the Gertrude bag in case she felt like making another escape attempt.

The guard sat down behind the desk. His big, puffy body sank into the chair as he rustled some papers around on the desk. After a while he looked up at us. He seemed tired.

He said, 'What's your story, then?'

I was like, 'W-what do you mean?'

The guard rubbed his forehead with one hand and jabbed his pen into the desk with his other. 'Why are the two of you on a train, alone, at night, with no tickets, and a live chicken?'

My mouth went dry. My brain whirled. I wondered if I was about to faint. I said, 'W-we have tickets. I just forgot to bring them, that's all. Once we get home, I'll post them to you.'

The guard smiled and rubbed his face. He said, 'Even if that were true, do you really think I'd just let you walk out of here on your own? How old are you, anyway?'

'S-sixteen,' I replied.

The guard sat back and barked out a single laugh. His chair creaked so much I thought it was going to shatter into a thousand pieces.

He said, 'Course you are,' proper sarcastically, suddenly snapping back into his normal position. 'Now, come on, give me your parents' phone number so they can come and pick you up.'

I shook my head.

He was like, 'Why? Are you orphans, or something?'

I said, 'No. It's just . . . complicated.'

'Complicated how?' he fired back. I could tell he was losing patience from how he was jackhammering that pen into the desk.

'Well, we don't know our mum's number and our dad doesn't have a phone.'

The guard laughed. 'Doesn't have a phone? Does he live in 1825 or something?'

'Kind of,' I said.

The guard held up his hand and said, 'I've heard enough. I'm calling the police.'

Mary gasped. So did I.

Then Mary gasped again.

I looked at her. She was holding her hand to her chest and wheezing and coughing.

I was like, 'Mary, what's the matter?'

'It's my assmar,' she croaked. 'I need my hailer.'

Wow. I tried not to smile, but this was genius. She was using the skills she learned from Oscar.

The guard sat forward and barked, 'Get her inhaler, then!'

I made a show of patting all my pockets down.

'Where is it?' I said as Mary's gasps got more and more desperate. 'I had it when I was on that train . . . Oh, I bet I know what happened. When your colleague was manhandling me, it must have fallen out of my pocket. This is all the train company's fault.'

Mary coughed and croaked. 'Ooooh, my longs hurt!'

The guard picked up his phone and dialled. 'Yes, I need emergency medical assistance in C2—come quick.' He pointed at me. 'Is there anything I can get for her?'

I said, 'Yeah, a glass of water. Cold. Very cold. You have to leave the tap running for a long time.'

The guard shot up and waddled to the back door as fast as he could. As soon as he was away, Mary stopped wheezing. She said, 'Did I do good, Nelson?'

I smiled. 'You did brilliantly—we would have failed the secret mission without you, now come on—quick.'

We leapt out of our seats and ran onto the platform. I knew we only had a minute until the guard came back. I shot a glance at the screen. The next train wasn't for another twenty minutes. There was no way we could wait that long without being seen.

We carried on along the platform and up the stairs into the main foyer. Smells from the fast food stalls made my stomach grumble but there was no way we could stop. Any minute now that guard would come after us.

I looked up at the signs. Buses and taxis this way. I thought getting a bus would be safer. Plus, I would probably be able to afford it. We trudged up the ramp to the bus area outside. The wind was freezing by now and a fine rain was falling. Mary put my coat back on and hugged herself to keep warm.

As if by magic, I saw a coach up ahead with 'Birmingham' on its display. There were people already on board and it looked like it was ready to go.

'Two child tickets for Birmingham, please,' I said to the driver.

'DON'T LET THEM ON!' The shout came from behind.

Oh no. I turned around and saw the security guard coming for us.

We jumped off the coach and belted through the concourse, dodging people, suitcases, and other obstacles.

'Stop!' the guard yelled at us. 'The police are coming!'

That just made me run quicker. To the right there was a slope leading under the station. It looked like some kind of car park. I dragged Mary down there while the guard was still quite a way behind us. When we got down there, I turned around and saw a big red button on the wall. CLOSE DOOR. I mashed it with my palm and carried on running. Even though I didn't look back, I heard the sound of the massive shutters coming down.

I looked around and realized that it was some kind of lorry loading bay. There was no way we could stick around because the guard saw us go down there. At the same time, if we left the station and went into Kings Lynn, they would probably find us there. We needed some other form of escape.

And that was when I saw it. An open lorry. On the side, it said, **J.M. SMYTHES—BIRMINGHAM**.

That'll do, I thought.

IS THIS OUR NEW HOUSE?

We huddled together next to some shelves right behind the driver's cab. We had no idea where we were or where we were going. We could only hope that the driver was heading back to Birmingham.

Luckily, there were bits of stock left in the back. I found a crate of bottled water and a box of crisps. We ate a bag each and crumbled up another for Gertrude. I have no idea whether chickens are supposed to eat crisps, but she wasn't complaining. I nearly fed her roast chicken flavour, but I thought that might be like cannibalism and gave her cheese and onion instead.

Mary fell asleep leaning against me and after a while, I must have dropped off, too, because the next thing I know, the lorry has stopped and the door is open.

'What's happening, Nelson? Are we at Mummy's?' Mary asked me.

I heard footsteps nearby.

I put my finger to my lips.

A voice asked if there was someone there.

We stayed silent.

He muttered something like, 'Must be going mad in my old age' and moved closer, walking quickly towards us, whistling softly. The hairs on my arms stood up. There was no way out of this one. The driver did a double take when he saw us, crouched down behind a box. He said, 'What are you doing in here?'

Something deep in my brain kicked in, as if I had been trained to do it. I jumped to my feet, hunched my shoulders, held my arms far apart, and roared.

The man jumped backwards, clutching his chest and I grabbed Mary and ran out of the lorry.

'Wait!' the driver called after us. 'Are you the Grizzly Dadams kids?'

I didn't have time to worry how he knew that, I just had to get away. We ran across the floodlit yard and out onto the main road. It was completely deserted. I scanned the area for houses or anything like that but there was nothing but the lorry place and loads of fields. The wind was so cold it bit through to my bones.

I squinted at a road sign.

It said 'Atherworth: 14 miles.' That was our old home town, where our old house was. That meant that Grundsford was about twenty miles away. There was no way we could get there at that time of night, though. We had to find shelter.

There was an old barn in the field opposite. It didn't exactly look luxurious, but it wasn't as if we had been living in a five-star hotel.

We crept inside and saw how run-down it really was. The roof was almost completely gone. The walls provided some shelter from the wind, but it was still freezing. Mary sat down and took Gertrude out of her bag and let her peck around on the floor. I knew we couldn't stay there too long or we would freeze to death. Without really thinking about it, I picked up a couple of dry sticks along with a small pile of hay and set about making a fire.

We sat around it, warming our hands and taking small sips of the bottle of water I found on the lorry.

Mary said, 'Nelson, is this our new house?'

I laughed and said, 'No, we're just going to wait here until it gets light, then we're going to see Mummy.'

Mary drew her knees close to her body and rested her head on them. Gertrude sat next to her.

Even though I was super uncomfortable, and there were probably rats scurrying around me, it had been such an exhausting day that I started to fall asleep, too.

CLUCKCLUCKCLUCKCLUCK

When I woke up the next morning, I felt like I had been frozen through like a Christmas turkey. I poked Mary with one of my blue fingers and woke her up and soon we were on our way.

It was still cold out, but the sun was bright, which seemed to take the edge off it. We walked along the side of the road in the long grass, getting splashed when passing cars sped through puddles.

I thought there had to have been a town or at least a village somewhere nearby, but there was nothing. It just looked like a never-ending road with the same scenery recycling itself over and over again—barn, road sign, squashed animal, barn, road sign, squashed animal. We managed about a mile before Mary started moaning. She was all, 'Nelson, I'm tired, my legs hurt, I want to sit down.'

I said, 'We can't sit down. We need to carry on so we can get to Mummy.'

She sighed dramatically like a diva and collapsed into the dirt. She said, 'I can't walk any more. I'm staying here.'

There is no changing Mary's mind once she gets like that.

After about ten minutes of piggybacking Mary along the muddy road, with a squirming Gertrude in the bag in my hand, I was ready to collapse. But then I saw it. The phone box.

I couldn't believe it. It was like seeing a dinosaur or something. I opened the door and was whacked in the face by the smell—an unholy mixture of mould and wee. It kind of reminded me of our outdoor toilet. I found an old business card, faded by the sun, stuck in the top of the phone—'AAA Taxis'. Brilliant. I fished a couple of coins out of my pocket, and ignoring Mary's moans about having to stand up, ordered the taxi.

After about ten minutes of standing in the stinky phone box as shelter from the wind, it arrived.

I said, 'Grundsford, please. Antonio's Hair Salon.'

The taxi driver grunted something and pulled away. I can't begin to tell you how nice it felt to sit on some comfortable car seats after a night in a barn. The radio played some old slow song and with the fields rolling by the window, I could feel myself gently falling asleep. I knew that when I woke up, I would be at Mum's.

Or so I thought.

'What the hell is that?' the taxi driver yelled.

My eyes snapped open. Gertrude was out of the bag

and flapping around the cab, sending feathers flying everywhere. Thinking about it, 'What the hell is that?' was kind of a stupid question. It was obviously a chicken.

I was like, 'Mary, why did you let Gertrude out?'

'She asked me to,' said Mary.

I stuffed Gertrude back into the bag and told Mary for what felt like the fifty jillionth time that chickens can't talk.

She said, 'Can too. "Cluck cluck cluuuuck" means, "I want to get out". "Cluck cluck" means "I'm hungry" and "cluckcluckcluckcluck" means—'

'HEY!' the driver slammed the brakes and looked at us proper fierce. 'Get out of my cab right now.'

The doors clicked unlocked.

I said, 'Oh come on, don't be like that. Look, the chicken is back in the bag and we're a couple of kids miles from home. You can't kick us out in the middle of nowhere.'

The driver sighed and turned around. He stared at us for a weirdly long time. It was really uncomfortable. He pulled his phone out of his pocket and squinted at it. Then he looked at us again. Then back at his phone. Then back at us. He whispered something under his breath. I gulped. There was nothing around. He was about to murder us and dump us in one of those fields and some poor dog walker would find us. I reached for the door.

CLICK. Locked again.

I said, 'Actually, I think we will get out.'

He was like, 'No, it's fine, I've changed my mind.'

He turned around and started driving.

I leaned forward and spoke into the little gap where you put your money and asked if everything was OK. He said 'Fine' again and then, 'Sorry about that, I've just never had a chicken in my cab before.'

I sat back. I noticed him adjusting his mirror.

The scenery slowly began to change. We passed through villages—each with its own little church and village shop. After a bit, the villages started to merge into one and post offices became shuttered-up take-away places. I nudged Mary when I saw the sign 'Welcome to Grundsford.'

'We're nearly there,' I whispered to her.

Mary grinned and clapped.

I looked out of the window. We were on the high street—it had all the same shops that Atherworth had, and a few extra ones. I could tell it was going to be a pretty good place to live.

I saw a sign up ahead—cream with posh black joined-up writing—Antonio's Hair Salon. 'It's just here on the right,' I said.

The driver didn't slow down.

I said, 'Did you hear me?'

He didn't respond.

I knocked on the partition. 'Hello?'

We coasted past the salon.

Mary yelled, 'Mr Driver, we want to get out now.'

We turned left into a car park. A big grey building was at the end of it. Above the door, in big, white letters, it said,

GRUNDSFORD POLICE STATION.

THREE DEEP BREATHS

The driver parked up and yanked the handbrake. Mary grabbed my hand.

I was like, 'Look, if this is about the chicken, I'm sorry. I'm going to pick up all the feathers before we leave.'

The driver turned around, looked me dead in the eye and said, 'I know who you are.'

'Huh?'

'Come on—out.' He unlocked the doors.

I said, 'I—I don't know what you're talking about.'

The driver said, 'You're the Grizzly Dadams kids. I need to turn you in.'

So that was why he was staring at us for so long. Panic shot through my body. I couldn't go in there. They'd put us into care or something. We'd end up in some home and I'd get beaten up by the other kids and Mary would grow up to be a psycho and then she would beat me up even worse than the kids in the home.

I was like, 'We're not the Grizzly Dadams kids. I don't even know who he is.' The driver was having none of it, though. I tried to calm Mary down, but inside, I was screaming.

255

We got out of the car. The driver stood there with his hands on his hips, saying, 'In you go.'

I looked him up and down. He was pretty small. Not much taller than me. And quite thin, too. He said, 'Move it.'

I took three deep breaths. My muscles went all tense and my fists clenched. He looked at me like I was crazy.

I took three more deep breaths then growled. Like a bear.

The driver actually looked scared. He went, 'You're as mad as your dad!'

I jumped forward and grabbed him in a bear hug.

He was screaming, proper screaming. Stuff like, 'Get off me, you crazy idiot! Police! Police!'

I put my leg behind his and gently lowered him onto the floor. I felt kind of bad, but you do what you have to do in the wild.

I bent my knees and straightened my arms. Mary screamed 'YAY' and jumped on for a very fast piggyback ride.

We belted down the road, the furious taxi driver not far behind us. I could see Antonio's in the distance. Mary bounced on my back and I gripped Gertrude's bag as tightly as I could.

I yanked Antonio's door open and jumped inside.

An old lady sitting with her head under a massive

dome screamed. This big bloke with an open shirt and a hairy chest, who I guessed must have been Antonio, stared at us and was all, 'Hey, what's going on here?'

The taxi driver tripped through the door and said, 'It's the Grizzly Dadams's kids. I need to take them in.'

A strange look passed over Antonio's face. He said, 'Nelson and Mary?'

We said yes.

He squatted down and put his hands on our shoulders. He said, 'Your mother's been worried sick.'

'Is she here?' I said.

He said, 'She's out searching for you.' He turned to a hairdresser watching from the other side of the room and told her to call my mum.

The driver wasn't satisfied and wanted to know what was going on. Antonio stood up and strode over to him and was like, 'Their mother is on the way. There is no need to take them anywhere.'

The driver wasn't happy at all. He said, 'Well, there's the small matter of my fare.'

Antonio pulled a massive wodge of notes out of his top pocket, peeled a few off the top, and pressed them into the driver's hand. He said to him, 'I trust that will be enough.'

The driver looked down and his eyes went proper bulgy. He said, 'Yeah, thanks mate,' and left super quick.

I said to Antonio, 'So does Mum work for you, or something?'

Antonio chuckled to himself and said, 'I think we should wait until she gets back before we answer any questions. Come on, let's get you sat down.'

He led us into a small lounge behind a 'staff only' door. It was the weirdest lounge I had ever been in—there was a lava lamp and a fake leopard-skin rug and incense sticks burning. He left us there while he went into the kitchen to make us drinks.

We sat down on the zebra print sofa and I put my arm around Mary. It had been a long and terrifying journey, but we had made it. We were finally safe.

The front door swung open, jingling the bell like mad. Heavy footsteps thudded through the salon and into the doorway. Mum stood there, her hands over her mouth. I didn't know what to do. She dropped her hands to her sides and walked in slowly. Her face was all puffy.

She said, 'My babies.'

THAT GREASY IDIOT

It's hard to explain what happened next. I mean, I was really happy about seeing Mum—it's what I had been working towards for months—but there was this nagging question in the back of my mind the whole time. It wouldn't leave me alone, no matter how much Mum hugged us and told us she loved us. In the end, I couldn't keep it in. I said, 'If you love us so much, why did you leave?'

Her face froze. She sat back and sighed, dabbing her face with a tissue. She said, 'I'm sorry, Nelson. I just couldn't cope any more. Your father and I were always arguing and there were so many things happening that I just had to get out for a while.'

That massive throat lump came back with a vengeance. I looked at the floor, focusing on the tacky rug, counting the black stripes. I said, 'You could have at least said goodbye.'

No one said anything. For ages. The only sound was Gertrude gently clucking. This wasn't how I pictured it in my head. In fact, I don't think I had pictured it. I was so fixed on finding Mum that I didn't think about what would happen when I did.

She said, 'It was too hard. I didn't think I would be able to explain how I felt. I couldn't bear to see you upset. I came in to see you while you were sleeping, the night before I left. I said goodbye then.'

I didn't know what to do. I couldn't look at her. I picked up a hairdressing magazine then put it straight back down. I glanced at Mary. She was leaning on Mum with her eyes closed. Mum was stroking her hair.

Mum leaned towards me a bit and whispered, 'Dad didn't hurt you, did he?'

I jumped up and snapped, 'No, he would never hurt us. He's not dangerous. He's just . . . I don't know what he is.'

I shocked myself that I was defending him, especially after I had run halfway across the country to escape him.

The front door of the salon swung open. I heard Antonio say, 'Easy, fella, we don't want no trouble.'

All I heard then was, 'WHERE ARE MY CHILDREN?'

Oh God.

Mum jumped up and stood in front of me.

'Daddy?' said Mary.

Mum said, 'Just stay there, sweetheart. Everything is going to be OK.'

Dad stormed into the room and stopped suddenly when he saw us. He looked worse than normal—the bits of his face not covered in hair were grey.

Mum gasped and said, 'Oh, Tim, what has happened to you?'

I guessed Mum must have known about the Grizzly Dadams videos, but seeing him in the flesh was a completely different experience.

Dad stomped across the room and looked down at us. His breaths were quick and shallow, his muscles all tensed. Suddenly he scooped me and Mary up and held us close.

He said, 'I'm sorry. I'm so sorry.'

I was like, 'Wait, why are you sorry? I put you on the internet and made the whole world laugh at you—and then I ran away.'

Dad put us down and sighed. He went, 'It is all my fault, I shouldn't have taken you away from home and sold all your things. I just wanted to give you a better life.' He stopped and rubbed his beard. 'I don't know what I wanted.'

Mum was all, 'You could have at least sent me your new address. You can't just take my children to the other end of the country and not tell me.'

Dad stood up and yelled, 'Oh, your children. Were they your children when you abandoned them for that greasy idiot you met on the internet?'

'Hey!' said Antonio.

Oh.

Oh.

So that's why Dad developed this sudden hatred for

261

the internet. Mum had met Antonio on it and Dad must have known about it. God, no wonder he thought everything electronic was evil—it had broken up his family. I bet me always playing online games with strangers made it worse, too.

Dad pointed at Antonio and said, 'Get out of here before I do something I regret.'

Mum got between them and said to Dad, 'See, this is your problem. You've always had a temper.'

Dad hissed, 'Only since I met YOU.' Then it descended into shouting again—squaring up to each other and pointing and saying horrible things. They had been away from each other for months and had picked up exactly where they left off. This wasn't what I wanted.

I said, 'Can you stop it, please?' They ignored me.

Mary said, 'Mummy, Daddy, stop shouting. You're upsetting Gertrude.'

They carried on as if they couldn't hear us. I tried asking them to stop again, but they didn't. I cried out, grabbed the lava lamp and smashed it on the floor.

That did it.

Antonio screamed, 'Hey, how am I supposed to create cool vibes, now?'

Mum and Dad stared at me. Weird blue stuff slithered all over the floor like ectoplasm.

I said to them, 'We are going to shut you in this room

together and you're not coming out until you've sorted everything out.'

'No way,' said Mum. 'You're not running away again.'

'As if you can lecture anyone about running away,' said Dad.

Mum yelled, 'Oh SHUT UP, Tim. I'm not the one who sold our house and went to live in the wilderness like that stupid Puma man!'

Dad was like, 'His name is Panther, you KNOW it's Panther.'

I said, 'We'll still be here when you're finished. And to prove we're serious, we'll leave you with Gertrude.'

Mary went to protest, but I managed to get her out of the lounge and back into the salon where a hairdresser and the old lady in the egg dome were trying to make it seem like they hadn't been listening to every word.

I could see a shape outside the glass door, pacing up and down. I went over to see who it was. I thought I had a good idea.

Antonio was like, 'Hey, stay where you are.'

I ignored him and opened the door.

Mary yelled, 'PWIMWOSE!!!!'

Primrose pulled us both in for a hug. This was amazing, I had never been hugged this much in my life. Maybe I should run away more often.

She asked if our parents were talking.

I said, 'Something like that. They might be a while, though.'

Primrose was like, 'I bet you guys are famished—shall we go and have breakfast?'

My stomach groaned. I felt like I hadn't eaten in days. I said, 'That would be AMAZING.'

Antonio tried to stop us but there was no way I was staying in there when a nice breakfast with Primrose was on the cards. As a compromise, Primrose gave him her phone number and told him to call when they were ready. He smirked and said, 'I'll call you any time, baby.' It was around then that I realized I probably wasn't going to be a big fan of this Antonio bloke.

REPORTED SIGHTINGS

We didn't talk much during breakfast. We were just focusing on getting food into our bodies. My God, guys, it was amazing. I mean, I'd had a full English before, but this was something else. After living on bran and porridge and horrible stinky fish for so long, it was literally like eating God's breakfast.

After I had sat for a moment and basked in the deliciousness of what I had just eaten,  I had questions—mainly about how Primrose and Dad found us.

She said, 'As soon as we'd found out you'd gone, we called the police. But I knew there was only so much they could do, so I uploaded a photo of the two of you to Facebook and Twitter and asked people to spread it around. The fact that you were the Grizzly Dadams's kids meant it quickly went viral.'

Mary looked up from the salt-and-pepper-shaker fight

she was creating and asked what viral meant.

Primrose said, 'It means loads of people saw your picture.'

Mary put the shakers down and said, 'So that means I'm famous?'

Primrose said, 'I suppose it does, Mary. By the way, I've brought you a present.'

Mary's eyes went massive as Primrose reached into her bag and pulled out a bangle. It was green and red and had 'Mary' scratched into it.

I could tell Mary loved it. She put it on and held it up to the light with a massive grin on her face. She even promised not to let Dad throw it away.

I asked Primrose if Dad was OK with her putting us on the internet.

Primrose took a sip of her coffee and said, 'Nelson, your father was so beside himself with worry, he would have done anything to get you back. Anyway, we soon started receiving reported sightings, in Norwich, Kings Lynn, Birmingham, all over. There were some mad ones which were obviously made up—this lorry driver claimed you roared at him like a bear.' She stopped and laughed.

I twirled my finger around my ear like this and went, 'Yeah, what a whacko.'

Primrose said, 'We started to follow the sightings and noticed they were heading towards Grundsford. So that's where we went. Thankfully, we were right. It seems like we were one step behind you the whole way.'

I glanced around the café. I could see people looking at us. It was weird. You know when celebrities say they want their privacy? I used to think that was a load of old rubbish, but I can totally see what they mean now. I asked Primrose if Dad was angry.

She said, 'Yes, but not with you—with himself. He's a good man, your dad, underneath it all. I've discovered that. He's far more than just Grizzly Dadams.'

I heard someone on the table next to us whisper, 'Ooh, she just said his name.'

We had planned to go for a walk around Grundsford afterwards, but all the looks we were getting were starting to freak me out so we headed back to the salon.

It was quiet when we got inside. That had to be a good thing. Unless they had murdered each other. I knocked on the door. Dad got up and opened it. Inside, Mum sat on the couch, clutching a mug of tea. Dad had one too. They both looked like they'd been crying. I looked away, at Gertrude pecking around on the floor. She had kind of messed up Antonio's rug.

Mum said, 'I think we're going to be OK, son.'

Dad nodded and said, 'We are.'

THANKS FOR WATCHING

Are you still here? Still listening to me? To be honest, I wouldn't be surprised if you'd bailed ages ago. I hear there's a wicked new video where a goat recites the alphabet. Thirty seconds long. Not over two hours. Still, if you have stuck around, thanks. I felt like I needed to get all this off my chest.

Anyway, what happened next? I bet you think that Mum left that sleazeball Antonio and that we all went back to our old house with Gertrude the chicken and lived happily ever after. Well, that's not exactly how it turned out.

Mum decided to stay with Antonio. She and Dad just fell out of love, and that's all there was to it. It's sad, but it is what it is. I don't really understand it, to be honest. How can you love somebody so much you'll marry them and have kids with them and then just stop? I don't know. Adults are weird.

So we went back to our house in Sheepy Murva, just the three of us. Well, four if you count Gertrude.

Now, I know what you're thinking: 'Are you mental? Why would you go back to that hellhole?' Well, it has changed.

Dad has, too. Primrose reckoned he had something called a 'wake-up call'—you know—where you realize that you've been acting like an idiot.

Don't worry—he's still Grizzly Dadams. He still grows stuff and whittles stuff and he still has a beard, but he's just toned it all down a bit. Notice how I've made this video in my bedroom instead of the stinky old outhouse? Look, if I move the camera— there's a TV in the corner—and an Xbox. My floor has a carpet. We have a TV downstairs where Mary can watch every episode of *Peter the Pirate* ever made.

As you guys know, Dad's even got into the whole YouTube thing, and as of now, he has filmed three 'Bushcraft with Grizzly Dadams' videos. The next one is about making your own water butts. He keeps saying stuff like, 'If you find that your butt is leaking, you must stick your hand in it and bung up the hole.' Yeah, you're going to love it.

Gertrude now has a world-class hen-house shaped like a pirate ship. Mary spends most of her time in there, sailing the seven seas and generally being crazy.

But best of all, better than anything ever, we have: IN . . . DOOR . . . TOILETS!

How nice it is to go to the toilet in the middle of the night and not get stuck to the seat with frost. When Dad got rid of the old one, he smashed it to pieces with a massive hammer. He let me have a whack at it too, which felt brilliant.

Anyway, as you probably know, Dad's whittling business is getting bigger and bigger—and yeah, a lot of it is because of his internet fame, but it wouldn't have happened without the great website Primrose made for him. He's getting more orders than he can handle and has had to take on a couple of apprentice whittlers on Sundays. Their names are Kirsty and Ash and they are annoyingly good at it. He even allowed Kirsty to make a Midlake Darston ornament and send it to him. When

Midlake showed it off on his video and said it was from 'Grizzly Dadams's cool friend Kirsty', she couldn't speak for a week.

As Dad is now internet famous, he has had numerous offers to take part in TV shows like *Curling with the Stars*, *Celebrity Prison*, and *Celebrity Nudist Camp*, but has turned them all down. He is happiest at home, whittling. Plus, come on, I don't want to see my dad naked.

Weekends are when Mum visits. We usually go for a day out somewhere. This once, we went down to the seafront because I wanted her to meet Scarfwick, but when we got down there, workmen were building a café. Apparently, since Grizzly Dadams, tourists have started to visit Sheepy Murva and they want to capitalize. Scarfwick is taking to it especially well, making the most of his appearances in the videos by offering 'Sweary Scarfwick's Boat Rides' for a fiver. That includes a Scotch egg too, so it's not a bad deal. Mrs Scarfwick used to help out sailing the boats, until she fell asleep at the wheel and they ended up in Amsterdam.

Primrose has been great since we came back—she is at ours most nights, helping me with my homework, maintaining the website, and sometimes just sitting with us and talking. The nights she takes over dinner from Dad are the best, too. My mouth is watering just thinking about it.

A lot of the time after dinner, Dad and Primrose will stay up in the kitchen with a bottle of this horrible home-made stuff from Dad's shed. When I turn the TV off, I can hear them talking and laughing. It's good to hear Dad laugh again.

It was brilliant to have my games back, too. I was allowed to use some of the money I earned to buy myself all the best gear. It was amazing. I waited until everything arrived before I sat down to play. But something weird happened.

I wasn't that excited.

I mean, don't get me wrong, I still love gaming, it's just not an obsession like it was before. Like, when I'm at school trying to sneak past a gang of bullies at the gate, I don't switch to spy mode in my head and act like I'm a game character. I don't pretend I'm playing games instead of living life any more. I just live it.

Last week, I actually started making my own game. Primrose is teaching me how to use this game creator as well as little bits of programming and I'm really getting into it. The game is called *Grizzly Dadams: Master of Bushcraft*. You play as Dad and complete the levels by making tools from naturally-occurring materials.

Dad is totally OK with the game, but did say that the only enemies should be the 'forces of Nature'. So I spent a whole day designing a Marshall Cremaine end-of-level boss for nothing.

Sometimes, I have to ask Dad about things for research, and he is always happy to point me in the right direction. I mean, the other day, I ended up sitting halfway up a tree with a pair of binoculars watching how blackbirds build their nests. And sometimes it is nice to just go for a walk in the woods and stuff like that, especially when you're not being forced to do it and you know you have a TV waiting for you at home.

Don't worry, I haven't gone fully outdoorsy—and if you ever catch me saying stuff like 'the bounty of nature', you have my permission to fire me out of a cannon, but I don't know, I guess I appreciate that kind of thing more.

And as strange as it sounds, I must have learned something from Dad. I mean, when we ran away, I built a fire, I made myself big like a bear, and I even squeezed the air out of a taxi driver's lungs. If he hadn't gone mad, we would never have survived when we ran away. Then again, if he hadn't gone mad, we wouldn't have run away in the first place.

Ugh, I'm rambling so I'm going to go. Thanks for watching my videos and commenting—even those people that call me a wuss and stuff even worse than that. And I know the whole reason I started this channel was to get my mum back and that hasn't really happened, but things haven't turned out too bad in the end. I was probably a bit stupid to think that a load of money would get our family back together. I guess when your mum runs off with a hairdresser off the internet and your dad turns into a crazier version of Panther Blimmington-Weltby, there isn't a YouTube video in the world that will change things back to normal. Not even that goat one.

Anyway, I'm off. The new café down by the harbour is opening tonight and me, Dad, Mary, and Primrose are guests of honour. Dad is cutting the ribbon and doing a speech, wearing a suit he made himself.

I'd better take the camera.

ACKNOWLEDGEMENTS

As anyone who has watched my videos will attest, I am definitely no YouTube expert, so I must thank Alex Barr and Luke and Nathan Jackson for lending their expertise during the writing of this book.

I should also thank our friends, Conrad, Claire, Charlotte and Joshua Jackson for unwittingly giving me the initial inspiration. The YouTube bit, not the mad dad bit.

ABOUT THE AUTHOR

As well as writing books, Ben Davis has had a variety of jobs, including joke writer, library assistant, and postman. Writing books has proven the most fun.

Ben lives in Tamworth, Staffordshire, and in his spare time enjoys rock climbing, white water rafting, and pretending to have adventurous hobbies.

ONE

If you're lost and have already used your compass to fight off an angry bear, simply follow the sun. If you've followed the sun and are still lost, use your sunburned face to attract the attention of passing aircraft.

TWO

You can tell a lot about the wildlife in the area by examining its droppings. If they are larger than a dinner plate and have fragments of clothing in them, consider leaving.

THREE

Forests can be very cold at night so you should huddle with your partner to keep warm. If you are travelling alone, you can construct a partner out of leaves, twigs, and dung.

FOUR

When fighting a crocodile, avoid the temptation to punch it in the mouth. That is exactly what it wants you to do.

FIVE

Desert mirages can play cruel tricks on the brain. Once, when trekking across Egypt, I thought I saw a McDonalds on the horizon. When I reached it, it turned out to be a Burger King.

SIX

When considering whether to eat wild berries, remember this rhyme:

IF IT'S RED, GO AHEAD. IF IT'S PURPLE ... DON'T.

SEVEN

In order to catch a fish, you must think like a fish.
Try to shorten the length of your short-term memory
to seven seconds.

EIGHT

In order to catch a fish, you must think like a fish.
Try to shorten the length of your short-term memory
to seven seconds.

NINE

I have never suffered any ill effects from eating
wild mushrooms, and neither has the three-legged
leprechaun that lives in my beard.

TEN

Travel light. Take only one bottle of water, one Swiss
Army knife, and the *Complete Panther Blimmington-
Weltby Survival Encyclopaedia Collection*
available now from all good retailers.

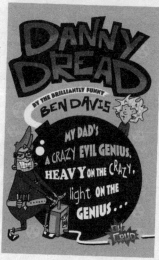

WHY NOT TRY ONE OF THESE OTHER FUNNY BOOKS . . .